MURPHY: COWBOY DECEIVED

THE KAVANAGH BROTHERS BOOK 6

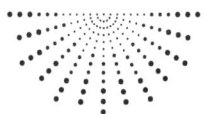

KATHLEEN BALL

Copyright © 2020 by Kathleen Ball

All rights reserved.

No part of this book may be reproduced in any form or by any electronic or mechanical means, including information storage and retrieval systems, without written permission from the author, except for the use of brief quotations in a book review.

❦ Created with Vellum

CHAPTER ONE

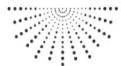

A ratcheting *click-clacket-click* sounded near Murphy's head and he woke with a start. That was a gun. His heartbeat thundered in his ears as he eased his gaze upward. Standing above him was an older man with long greasy hair and an unkept beard. His clothes were ragged, and he smelled as though he never bathed.

"Mister I'm not looking for any trouble," Murphy said as he slowly sat up. The heaviness of the gun in his hand hidden under the blanket felt good. "I'm just traveling through. If you like, you can share my breakfast."

But the offer didn't affect the old coot who kept his gun trained at Murphy's chest. "You're not here to steal land?" The man's eyes narrowed.

"No, sir. I have a legal matter, and then I'm heading back to my ranch in Texas. I have enough work to do with my spread. I sure don't need any more land."

The man stared at him for more than a minute and then uncocked his gun. He put it back in his holster. "Name is Crier, Jim Crier. Everyone just calls me Crier."

Murphy stood and strapped on his holster. He put out his

hand. "I'm Murphy Kavanagh." They shook hands, and Murphy suppressed his cringe, hoping none of the vermin on Crier jumped onto him. Murphy stepped back and quickly revived the waning fire. It didn't take him long to make coffee and heat a can of beans. "Help yourself."

Crier dug in. Since there was only one fork and one cup Murphy waited. Crier scooped the meal right out of the skillet, slurping and swallowing with an occasional grunt, not stopping until three-quarters of the beans were gone. Licking his lips, he held out the skillet to Murphy.

"Go ahead and eat the rest," Murphy said, shaking his head. "I need to pack up." He really wanted to scrub everything Crier touched. He could make more coffee later.

Shrugging, the older man went back to shoveling the food into his mouth, and from the look of it, Murphy wouldn't have a long wait to get his utensils back.

"This is the Hills Plantation area, isn't it?" he asked softly.

"What's left of it. The area didn't survive the war much and people mostly left." Crier scraped the last beans up and handed the skillet to Murphy. "Thanks for the grub. I'm hoping the missus is done cooking my food. Take care now."

Murphy released a sigh and then chuckled after Crier was out of earshot. He'd been sure the old man was there to rob him. He set the skillet aside, planning to rinse it out before he stowed it. Then Murphy had one stop to make before he headed to town. The entire time he had traveled from Texas to Arkansas, all he could think about was *her*. He'd privately mourned her these last years. She still had his heart, and he didn't know what to do about it. He supposed he would soon find out if there was anything that *could* be done about it.

He'd been getting hints about getting married from his nine brothers and their housekeeper, Dolly. For the most part, he ignored their pointed comments, but he'd have to tell them the truth soon before they sent off for a bride. They didn't know about his marriage, didn't know that his heart was still taken. He'd never love another the way he'd loved Brooke.

As soon as he had cleaned up, he lifted himself onto the saddle. "One more stop, Nugget," he told his palomino. He took a few moments and got his bearings, then rode north. Before he knew it, he was in more familiar territory. As he approached the area behind what was once Brooke's family home, he jumped down and walked.

The willow tree still stood and was just as majestic, its yellow branches trailing down, seeming to weep over the land below it. A smile tugged at his lips. He'd had a few memorable picnics under that tree with Brooke.

He tried to harden his heart against the memories, but it was too late. The pain of losing her was as fresh as when he had first been given the awful news. He stood in front of a big light-colored rock. It was the only marker of her grave.

He had ridden in, beat and beleaguered, the war finally over, and he wanted only to see his wife. Thoughts of her, of holding her in his arms had given him the energy to return home. But his father-in-law had met him at the property's edge and taken him to the rock.

"Brooke is here," the old man had said bitterly, showing she had been buried under that cold piece of granite.

"What? No!" Anguish, hot and heavy, had rolled over him. "What happened?"

But her father had only shaken his head, unable or perhaps unwilling to give an answer. "There's nothing here for you now," the old man had grunted out. "Best you be on your way."

"Let me carve her a proper marker," Murphy'd begged, tears rolling down his face.

"No need," her father had answered with grim resolution. "Those who love her know where she is."

"Let me stay, help you rebuild the farm," Murphy had suggested, desperate to stay close to Brooke, to the place where he had felt her love and warmth.

Her father was a stubborn old coot, though, and he had jutted out his chin in defiance. "Best you just go back where you came from," he'd said, and then he'd turned his back and shuffled away, shoulders stooped.

There had been no other choice. Heartbroken, somehow Murphy and Nugget had made it home. He just had never been able to bring himself to tell anyone he'd been married; the pain of talking about it was too much. His family thought his bouts of sadness and anger were remnants of the war. And God help him, he had let them hold to that belief.

Glancing at the house now, he cringed. It wasn't standing quite square anymore. It looked to be leaning on one side. There wasn't a crop in the field, just dried soil that was mostly overgrown with grass and weeds. A garden struggled for survival to the rear of the house, though, and it looked like someone had tried to keep it tended. There were a few animals wandering about, so someone must have been feeding them or they would have left. A kind neighbor, perhaps… or squatters. Hopefully, selling the land and animals would be easy. First, though, he needed to talk to the lawyer.

Murphy turned Nugget and headed for town. It was a small town, and he didn't even know its name, though he vividly remembered the battle of Hills Plantation…

They had all been so young and full of themselves, he and his men, especially the first day when they had driven the Union Army a quarter mile back. They'd felt invincible, but that feeling hadn't lasted very long. The Yankees had come after them and whooped them good. But just driving the Confederate Army back wasn't good enough. They had started hunting down rebel soldiers.

So many of his company had been slaughtered. With a lead ball in his shoulder, Murphy had hidden and, at his first chance, had hightailed it out of there. It was a miracle he'd slipped past. He hadn't stopped at the closest farm, figuring it was too great a risk that he'd get caught. It had taken him four pain-filled days to get to the Malery Farm.

He'd been so thirsty, but too afraid to go to the Cache River. Shots seemed to come from that direction rather frequently. When he spotted a house, he stayed hidden in the woods until nightfall. Under cover of the darkness, he drew water from the well and then sheltered in the barn. It'd been all too common for soldiers to hide in the hay, so it was often the first place searched. He couldn't risk that. No, he needed something clever. He studied the barn and, despite the pain in his shoulder, spent all night digging. He was right proud of his hiding spot.

He'd dug under the water trough, a hole big enough and long enough for him to crawl into, where he would be unseen. The only bad part was the pile of manure mixed with hay he used to cover himself. But he had to do what he had to do. Settling in, he got some rest, and occasionally left the safety of his hole to watch the people in the house.

His breaths came sharp and fast, and his heartbeat quickened as Nugget tossed his head, returning him to the present as he rode into the tiny town. The war was past, he reminded himself. He didn't have to hide any longer, and he sure didn't want to remember. It was better to put his past behind him.

Murphy reined Nugget in at the lawyer's office and swung out of the saddle. The building was hardly more than a large shed made of wood. To anyone else, its appearance would probably not intimidate. He took a deep breath. It was going to be an interminable day.

The door creaked as he opened it and stepped across the threshold. As his eyes adjusted to the dim light, he belatedly remembered to take off his hat. An older woman in a worn but clean dress glanced up from her desk just inside the door but said nothing. A man about his own age sat behind a scarred and battered desk inside a small room off the main one. He rose and approached Murphy, holding out his hand.

"I'm Tom Faber," said the man as he and Murphy exchanged a handshake. "Are you Murphy Kavanagh?"

Murphy studied the man, trying to decide if he looked familiar, as he gave a brief nod.

"I'm glad you could make it. You have plenty of decisions to make." He gestured to the small side room. "Come into my office; we can have a bit of privacy."

Plenty of decisions? What was that supposed to mean? Murphy hoped to start his return trip that afternoon.

"Everything is pretty straight forward," Faber continued, indicating Murphy should take one of the seats in front of his desk. "We're just waiting on one other person."

The outside door opened and closed. The footsteps on the wooden plank floor sounded light, like a woman's. Murphy turned in his chair to see who it was. His breath left his lungs in a whoosh and the blood ran out of his face. He shook his head, thinking he might be hallucinating. A lump formed in his throat as his heart felt as though it was being squeezed in an ever-tightening vise.

"Hello, Murphy," said the newcomer in a brisk tone. "Tom, let's get to it."

Murphy stared at the redheaded woman, stunned and speechless. She hadn't changed a bit. But how could this be happening? Finally he recovered his breath enough to speak. "But… you're dead. I was even shown where you were buried."

One eyebrow quirked upward. "And yet here I am… where I've always been, Murphy. While I waited for a husband who never came home. Tom?" She took a seat on the chair next to Murphy. Her fresh scent washed over him as she passed, and he inhaled deeply, still struggling with his shock.

"I had to check a few things out since Mr. Kavanagh deserted you. I was hoping things would go your way, Brooke. Unfortunately, since he is your husband, the land belongs to him." Tom looked at Brooke as though he pitied her.

Brooke closed her eyes as she nodded. "I had a feeling this was how it would play out. I've got a job lined up."

"Doing what?" Tom asked.

"Laundry. It'll do until I can move on to something else. I doubt living in a tent in the winter will work. Maybe if I could get a divorce, I could find a husband who doesn't run from responsibility. I need someone I can count on. Someone who won't deceive me to get what he wants." Tears glistened in her eyes as she stood. "Thank you, Tom." She turned and stared at Murphy. "I'll pack up and be off the property by tomorrow." She put her hand over her heart for a moment, then squared her shoulders and walked out.

Murphy stared after her as a sense of coldness swept through him. *She's alive.* The words kept echoing through his mind. *How? What happened?* Her statement began registering. She thought he'd never come back for her?

His chair toppled as he leaped to his feet, but he left it lying on its side as he ran from the office and vaulted into his saddle. "We need to catch up with her, Nugget."

She was already out of sight, but he knew where she was going.

CHAPTER TWO

Brooke's hands trembled as she tried to hold the reins. She veered off her path and took the road to the Cache River. She reined in and slipped down off the saddle. Her heart pounded madly against her ribs. *What just happened? Why did Murphy come back?* From what she'd been told, he was a rich rancher. Why would he want her failing farm? When she had ridden into town, she'd expected Tom Faber to have a telegram stating that Murphy wanted nothing to do with the land. She'd *counted* on it.

When he had abandoned her after the war, she'd never thought to see him again. She'd held out hope for months that he would change his mind and come back for her, but he never had. What he had done had turned her bitter toward all men. Not that it mattered. In the eyes of the law, she already had a husband and wasn't allowed to find a new one. Without a mate, she'd been torturously lonely. She had spent night after night wondering what had been lacking in her that had made him run off and leave her behind.

And now Murphy was back.

What had he been doing for the past eight years? Had he pretended he wasn't already married and married another?

She couldn't imagine him living without a woman. It didn't seem in his nature to be alone. Oh, how she'd been taken to task by her father for marrying Murphy. He'd warned her that men like Murphy Kavanagh were no good, and when her husband had abandoned her after the war, her father hadn't let her forget her poor choice in a man. It had been difficult to hold her head up all these years. She'd loved Murphy more than life. She'd poured every ounce of love in her heart into him. She had known he could die in the war, and she'd prayed and prayed every day for him, yearning for the day he would finally come home and sweep her into his arms. She had been convinced once he did everything would right itself, her father would see how good a man Murphy was.

But he hadn't come for her.

Brooke walked along the river, her eyes full of tears and her heart full of anger. She'd waited and waited for him to come home. When he never arrived, she had mourned him as dead. It wasn't until she told her father she would need to find another husband, someone who could help with the farm, that he finally admitted to her that Murphy was alive. His disclosure had left her reeling. The hurt had been an immense blow, both physically and emotionally.

"I told you he was a no-account," her father had admonished. "Now you need to buck up and realize you've been played the fool. That man got what he wanted from you and left. He probably never looked back."

That experience had changed her. She'd always been happy, quick to laugh, eager to be around friends. But not anymore. She had gone into isolation and kept to herself. All that had mattered was her family and the farm. She had nothing to offer anyone else.

One by one, her friends got the message and the men who'd been waiting to hear she was a widow let her be. At least when she was home, she didn't have to pretend everything was just fine. No one said a word when she sometimes cried herself to sleep. She was strong and did as much as she could to work the farm. She always tried to do her best, but somehow, she knew her best would never be good enough. She'd hoped to keep going, just like she always did.

It hadn't turned out that way.

She impatiently brushed away her tears and kicked a stone out of her path. Maybe if she'd been prettier, or better educated, he'd have come back. She'd been a fool and had taken his every look and touch to heart. Why hadn't she known better?

Her father had kept telling her to forget the man who had left her behind. But how could she even for a single day? Her son MJ was his very image. A handsome boy, to be sure. MJ was the only reason she still knew how to love. Otherwise she'd have withered.

As soon as she heard the bushes rustling, she knew he was approaching, and she turned back to the river. Even as she had stormed out of Tom's office, she had known Murphy would follow her there. How long and often had she thought about this moment? So many times... at first how wonderful it would be to tumble into his embrace, but then as the months turned into years and bitterness had filled her heart, she had pictured a very different encounter, one that involved the choice words she'd have for him.

But now... it was only hurt she felt, and shame that colored her every thought.

"Brooke," he whispered. "I was told you were dead."

She stiffened but didn't turn around. "My father warned me you'd say that if you ever came back around. How right he was." She wrapped her arms around her middle. She wasn't prepared for Murphy's lies.

"I came to the farm right after the war ended." His words came out forcefully, showing a sense of desperation as he spoke. "I planned to either stay and farm if that was what you wanted or take you to my family's ranch. Your father—" abruptly, he lowered his voice, spoke in a hushed, pain-filled tone. "Your father showed me your grave. I offered to stay and help him with the farm, but he told me to leave."

Slowly she turned, steeling herself. He was so very handsome, and his eyes implored her to believe him, told her he was truthful, but his eyes lied. She knew he *wasn't* being truthful. She was gullible when it came to this man. "You can save your lies, Murphy. There are two graves on the property. One is my mother's and the second is my father's. Just where is *my* supposed grave?"

"Under the willow tree," he answered with a hint of a tremor. "There's a big, almost white rock. Your father took me there."

What utter nonsense he spoke! "Go away, Murphy." Her voice quavered as she trembled. "My father wouldn't have done such a thing. Why would he have told you I was dead? He never would have allowed me to mourn for you as long as I did. He only discovered the rotten truth when I decided to marry again. No…" She shook her head as bitter tears stung her eyes. "You went right to your ranch and forgot about the woman you married. You forgot about me." Her tears spilled over and trailed down her face.

"I can't say why your father would have done such a cruel thing," he said softly. "But he did. He told me you had died, told me to go on back to my family. I mourned you too, Brooke. I haven't looked at another in eight years." He sighed. " I'll be back soon, and we can talk."

She laughed. "Like you did last time? Don't bother." She

ran to her horse and pulled herself up onto the saddle. Without a backward glance, she urged her mount toward the trail as fast as she could.

Murphy set up camp that evening at the edge of the woods just outside the border of her property. On a little hill he could see the house below, and he hoped she could see him from there. His plan had been to go right back to the ranch, but all his plans had fallen aside. Now he wanted her to see he was sticking around. He *had* returned to her after the war, and by gum he needed to convince her he was telling the truth.

Her father... he'd told Murphy Brooke was dead. Hadn't he?

"Brooke is here... Those who love her know where she is... Best you leave..."

A chill washed over Murphy as he replayed the old man's words in his head. Had he actually used the word "dead"?

So her father had sent Murphy away, apparently told Brooke that he'd never come back for her, never intended to honor their marriage. Her father was to blame for their circumstances. Why? Why destroy his daughter's marriage?

He shook his head. There was no understanding it. Murphy'd never gotten on with Andy Malery. Brook's father had hated him from the first. The old man had always been afraid Murphy would take Brooke to Texas after the war. Murphy'd known it, but he never would have thought the hatred ran that deep. So deep the old man would lie to them both to keep them apart... to keep Brooke on the farm with him. His anger at the old man melted into sadness at all he and Brooke had missed out on.

There had been something special between them from the first moment they'd laid eyes on one another.

Murphy had been wounded not too far from the farm. He'd taken shelter there, and Andy had tried to get him to move along, off his property. Thank God for Brooke. She had saved his life.

She'd also kept him alive while he'd been away after his injuries healed. Knowing he would go back to her had kept him going, kept him safe.

For eight years... thinking she was dead. He'd been a broken man, barely able to function... And now, finding out she lived, she'd been alive all these years.

He wanted to hug her and kiss her and hold her. He needed to hear about her life since he had last seen her. She was his wife... He felt the shock of seeing her from head to toe. He had mourned her for so very long it had become part of him. It had been hard to hide his grief from his family, but he'd managed because he hadn't been ready to talk about his wife... his loss.

As he watched the house and yard below, the front door opened and a dark-haired boy came out. He jumped down each step and raced into the barn. There was no mistaking that thick head of walnut brown hair, so like his own. Even the way the boy carried himself.

It had to be.

Murphy could hardly breathe. His heart pounded, and his chest hurt more than ever. He had a son. He had a son and he hadn't known. *Why?* Anguish filled him. He wanted to scream to the heavens. Brooke must have hidden herself and the boy when he'd come around and had her father tell him she was dead. Had she decided she didn't want to be married to him? So she'd deceived him for eight years.

Murphy had watched too many of his friends die in battle, and each one had been a painful experience. And then he had thought his wife dead and that had been twice as tortuous, but this… hiding his child—his son from him was the worst betrayal he'd ever felt in his life.

Staring at the barn door, he waited for the boy to come back out. He impatiently swiped at his moist eyes. Why had she never sent word to him about the child's birth? What… *why?* Had he done something so wrong that she felt she could never forgive him? That he deserved to be punished? He'd believed in their love. But he'd been told she was dead.

He could call himself stupid now, and maybe some would, but he'd had no way of knowing that Brooke was alive.

The boy came out of the barn and froze, then turned and stared at Murphy for a moment. His eyes narrowed as though he were trying to figure something out. Then he scurried into the house.

Murphy had watched his nieces and nephews grow. He knew for a fact how much he had missed by not being in his son's life. Did his son think him dead or did he think he was abandoned? Had Brooke simply not loved him the way he loved her? She'd mentioned mourning him, yet when she found out he was alive… Why had she done nothing?

Despite his stomach churning, he built a fire. He didn't need it to cook; he just wanted her to know he was staying. He'd always lived a moral, honorable life. He believed himself to be a good Christian. Why hadn't she at least sent him a letter about his child?

"Ma, who is that man out there? He's set up camp," MJ asked.

Brooke swallowed hard. "He's a soldier I once met. I'm sure he'll be moving on soon. How about we have some supper and then I'll read to you for a bit?"

MJ smiled. "That's a good idea. Ma? Do you miss

Grandpa? I miss him something awful. Today would have been a good day for us to go fishing together. He liked to fish."

"He sure did." A smile tugged at her lips. "Especially when he was fishing with you. And yes, I do miss him very much."

MJ chattered throughout supper, but Brooke couldn't keep her mind off Murphy. All he'd done these last years was keep her from finding another husband. She should have contacted him and asked for a divorce, but her pride hadn't allowed it. And now... her pride had lost her the property that should have stayed in her family. Since they were still married, her inheritance had become his. A sigh slipped out. She'd need to pack up soon.

He must have known she was alive. That drivel he was spouting about her father saying she was dead, showing him a *rock*. It made no sense. What reason would her father have for doing such an awful thing? By the time the war had ended, it had been a struggle to keep MJ fed. Her father never would have turned away her son's father. No, he must have seen the condition of the farm and just left. How had he expected them to survive? She touched her threadbare and patched dress. It was decent only in that it kept her properly covered, but she made do. Somehow her pa had always made sure MJ had clothes and shoes that fit. They weren't new, but that hadn't mattered. Every penny they'd made had gone to the farm, though there had been precious little to put into the land over the last few years. And now even that was no longer hers.

After reading for a while, she tucked her yawning boy into bed. The house was too quiet, and the loneliness she constantly carried felt as though it was strangling her. Murphy had to have some agenda, but she couldn't think of what he was up to. Maybe he wanted to take MJ back to the ranch. The pounding of her heart drummed in her ears. There was no one left to help her. So many had died and the rest moved. When she'd buried her father, there were very few people left to attend.

Her thoughts drifted to the man who was still her husband. Murphy still looked so very handsome. He'd made it through the war. At first when she'd found out he was alive; she'd come up with so many reasons why he couldn't make it back to her. Maybe it had been fanciful thinking, but it had kept her sane. The notion he'd been too injured and couldn't get to her had been part of her thinking for so long. She had watched the road thinking any day she would spot him walking along it, that he would see her and drop everything and run to her. Too many notions and excuses had filled her head, but none of them true.

He wasn't the fun, smiling, loyal, loving man she'd married. Or maybe he had been once... but people changed, and he had changed for the worse. The Murphy she'd fallen in love with, the man she'd married, was gone.

Restless, she eased from the bed. Tea sounded like a good idea. Wandering into the kitchen, she put water on to boil. The window was too much of a temptation. It would hurt, but she looked. Murphy was out there, but she'd already known that. Seeing his fire made her stomach contract painfully. He wanted her son. That must be it. Well, she'd fight him tooth and nail about that.

And just maybe, while she was at it, she should fight him for her land. Why should *she* have to leave what should have been her birthright? Let that no-account man go back to Texas and leave the land to her.

The water boiled, but she didn't want tea anymore. She moved the pot from the stove to the counter and then banked the fire. Spring planting would need to be done and soon. It was doubtful she and MJ could handle it alone, but by golly she had no intention of leaving, despite what she had said in Tom's office. Now that her mind was made up, she had no choice but to do the plowing and planting. God would see them through. Her faith was powerful.

CHAPTER THREE

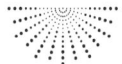

Brooke wiped her forehead with her sleeve. It was awkward since she didn't dare stop the plow. It was too hard to get Maisy going if they stopped. The rows weren't as straight as her father's had always been, but there were rows. Her major crop was wheat. That was her money crop. She'd also planted many vegetables to sell. That was her "we need to eat and buy supplies" crop. Spring always cheered her, but it was also an in-between time. Food wasn't plentiful on the farm.

She'd been at it for more than an hour and her back and arms already hurt something awful. Her shoulders burned, and she would have thought they were being pulled out of their sockets. From the corner of her eye, she glimpsed Murphy coming her way.

Heaving a sigh, she reined in the horse. "Whoa, Maisy," she called out and stopped the plowing. She waited until he got closer and then pulled her revolver out of her pocket and pointed it at him.

"Get off my property you low down… Just get off," she growled. It was one of her better growls.

"I want to help," he said with a shrug. "I would have offered when you started, but I know how stubborn you can be. When I noticed you were slowing, I figured you'd be happy for the help." His stare unnerved her. He wasn't afraid of her gun or her growl.

He took another step closer.

"You're stepping on my plowed rows," she snapped. "Even you should know better." It didn't matter, though, not really. He could stand there all day if he wanted. She put the gun away and jiggled the reins. "C'mon, Maisy."

With a jolt, the horse began pulling the plow again.

"If you come home to the ranch with me, you wouldn't have to do so much work." He walked right next to her, pesky as a fly. "Or if you have your heart set on staying here, let me help."

"Now why would you want to do that?" she grumbled.

He angled a look in her direction but kept walking. "I've been trying to work everything out in my head, and I can't figure out why your father told me you were dead."

Again with that horrid story. She huffed out a breath in exasperation. "Did you get shot in the head? Maybe you hit it against a rock? Thrown from a horse? Trying to work things out in your head isn't working." She kept going.

He stopped walking, and she smiled. At last. But his stride was long, and he caught up fast. "You know, I remember you as a sweet kind woman."

"You must be remembering wrong."

He stumbled over one of the uneven furrows. "Tarnation, woman! Can you stop so we can talk?"

"No." She'd never admit it, but she was enjoying their banter.

"Ma!" Her heart constricted as MJ ran their way.

"I know he's mine," Murphy said in a low voice, but try as

she might, she could not detect any malice or threat in his tone.

Still, best to be careful. "Prove it. He could be the child of one of many beaus I've had." Realizing what she'd just said, her face heated. "That didn't come out right."

"I know you're a God-loving woman. You'd never be that way," he said tenderly.

"Can I help too?" MJ asked as he came up to them out of breath.

"Sweetheart I will need you when we plant. This plow is too heavy for even me. Could you clean out Maisy's stall for me?"

MJ frowned as he began walking next to Murphy. "Why are you bothering my ma?"

"I just wanted to help. Look how tired she is," Murphy said.

"MJ."

"I'll go clean the stall," he said in a disappointed voice. He raced back to the barn.

Now she couldn't see where she was going; her eyes were filled with tears. Finally, she stopped and swallowed a sob. "You weren't here for MJ all these years, so don't think you can use him to get to me." She put her hands on her hips.

"What does MJ stand for?"

Her mind came up blank, so she shrugged. "I just like the letters is all." She closed her eyes, trying to stem her tears, but it didn't work.

"Brooke…" he said on a sigh. "I want to hold you and tell you everything will be fine. I know you won't let me, but please let me do just one thing for you. Go on inside, and I'll finish the plowing." His voice was incredibly gentle, and it made her feel soft inside.

She studied him for a moment, taking in his healthy,

muscled body, his clothing that was obviously used for work but was in better condition than her finest Sunday dress. He had a powerful jaw, but his features were soft, with kindness lighting his eyes. Overcome with emotions she couldn't name, she whirled about and ran to the house. Her tears would not stop, and she didn't want him to know how much she hurt.

As much as she wanted to start over, to believe his story, she just couldn't. Throughout her entire life, her father had never lied to her, and she couldn't trust Murphy's story. He was up to something... but what? They had rushed into a wedding. She'd hardly known him when they married. Her heart had been overflowing, and with his return to the war looming, it had seemed like their only choice. But she should have waited.

PLOWING WAS HEAVY WORK, definitely not fit for a woman; her arms must be screaming. At least she hadn't put up too much of a fuss and was allowing him to plow for her. It might be a small start, but it *was* a start. He couldn't get the grin he was wearing to disappear. MJ was his son. Brooke hadn't denied it. Did MJ stand for Murphy John? Or maybe he was Murphy Junior. It didn't matter. She'd as good as admitted he was the boy's father.

He'd missed so much. The boy's birth, his first words, first steps... teaching him about hunting and fishing and farming... ranching.

Even with Brooke's father not approving of him, Murphy still could not understand why the man had taken such a drastic step as to make sure his daughter remained without a husband, his grandson without a father. Though they had never gotten on well, the old man had always been civil. A frown pinched Murphy's forehead. Had he done something wrong? Why had her father taken such a dislike to him?

It must have been awful for Brooke, thinking her husband didn't want her. Had her father not cared how much he was hurting her to lie like he had? Had she spent all these years thinking he wanted someone else? Anger rushed through his veins, heating him into a fury. He was tempted to take the plow and dig up the old man. Even from the grave, her father was still interfering in his life.

He turned Maisy to make another row. He'd been so feverish when Brooke had found him in the barn. He had escaped detection from the Union Army hiding in that hole he'd made, but he'd been there three days, weakened by his injury, unable to adequately clean it so infection had begun to set in. He had thought Brooke was an angel at first, but as soon as her father joined her, he knew better. Even then, the old man hadn't wanted to help him. Andy Malery had told Brooke to leave Murphy there to die. Luckily, she hadn't listened.

Brooke had been so kind and caring as she nursed him, her touch gentle and soothing. She even took the bullet out of him. Her father made a few spiteful remarks to her, but she'd ignored him. She'd just call him grouchy.

Murphy and Brooke got to know each other those three weeks while he healed. Their relationship was easy and quickly turned into an attraction which developed into love. A love so deep he'd mourned her absence while he was off fighting. When the war was finally over, he'd been elated and excited to see his wife. He had looked forward to starting their life together. What a fool he'd been. He should have asked more questions when he'd finally arrived at the farm. He should have asked for details; Andy Malery hadn't even told him how Brooke had supposedly died, and Murphy hadn't questioned. He should have been suspicious. All he'd been was an idiot.

He needed to go back to town soon and send his family a letter. Wouldn't they be surprised by his news? They would probably be hurt too that he didn't tell them about Brooke from the start. He wished he could tell them when he would be coming home, but he didn't know what his plans were. He just wanted to be with Brooke and MJ. So far, his wife hadn't been very inviting. She didn't understand he had also suffered. His heart had broken into so many pieces he had never been able to put them all back together.

And now it was the distance and mistrust between them that hurt. He hadn't realized she could be so ornery. What had happened to her sweetness? He had once lived for one of her smiles. But now it looked like she saved her smiles for their son.

Speaking of whom, the boy was barreling full-tilt toward him. He'd been happy Brooke hadn't denied MJ was his, but in truth she really couldn't have. His son looked a lot like him. She'd raised the boy alone. It must have been hard to be a lone parent.

"Mister! Ma says you're to put Maisy away, clean up and have supper with us. Don't forget to wash behind your ears!" He lowered his voice and met Murphy's eyes with a solemn gaze. "She checks." He didn't wait for a reply, though, just ran back to the house.

Murphy smiled; he'd be sure to wash behind his ears. No sense in getting his wife riled.

OH MY... had Murphy always been so tall, so strong looking? The kitchen was too small with him in it. She glanced at him, and his wicked blue eyes twinkled. The same twinkling eyes that had helped to convince her to marry *him*.

"Mister, are you stayin' a while? My grandpa died and Ma gets so tired farmin'."

Brooke caught her breath. "MJ," she warned.

Murphy dropped to one knee. "Call me Murphy, and yes I do plan on staying a while… for as long as it takes." Then he reached out and ruffled MJ's hair.

"As long as what takes?" MJ's eyes were wide. He was expecting an answer.

Murphy turned to Brooke, but she shrugged her right shoulder and continued to slice the bread. Her heart plummeted. What if he told MJ Murphy was his father who walked away from her and never come back until now?

"Go wash up, MJ," she said instead.

"Aw Ma, I'm washed already."

"Even behind your ears?"

MJ glanced at Murphy and they shared a smile. This would never do. They could not become friends. MJ must never know the truth of Murphy's identity… and his betrayal.

"Help me set the table, please." Why had she invited Murphy for supper? She couldn't have been sane when she did it.

He easily set up three places at the table wearing a half-smile that tugged at her heartstrings.

She set the warm dishes in the center of the table and then they all sat and held hands to say grace.

"Lord, we do thank you for this food and the blessings of comfort and fellowship as we eat," said Murphy. "Amen."

Heart racing, Brooke snatched her hand back. It just wasn't right to get warm feelings while saying grace.

"Fried chicken, my favorite," Murphy remarked, shooting her a grin.

"It's mine too!" announced MJ. "Ma never makes it enough times."

"MJ, remember not to talk with your mouth full."

Subdued for the moment, MJ glanced at her and nodded and then watched Murphy. Long ago, she'd dreamed of such moments. Now one had come, and it pierced her heart.

Loud thunder rumbled overhead, and rain came on fast and heavy. "This storm certainly snuck up on us," she said.

Murphy stood quickly and wiped his face with a napkin, then pushed his chair back in. "I apologize, but I need to go get Nugget. He's not good in storms." Murphy tugged open the door and stepped out of the house and into the gushing rain.

"Come on MJ, put your coat on and we'll help with Murphy's belongings."

MJ jumped out of his chair and grabbed his coat. Then he also raced out into the pouring rain. She grabbed her wrap and followed, though it didn't do much to keep her dry. They ran across the property toward the camp. Murphy yelled something to them, but the wind carried his words away.

They grabbed his bedroll, coffee pot, a skillet, and a few cans of beans. Lightning lit up the sky. It looked as though it was putting cracks into the sky. An enormous boom exploded in the air, and Brooke's heart raced. This storm was a bad one. "Let's get back!" she shouted.

She made sure MJ was in front of her. He was running too fast to look back. Suddenly she was lifted and flying through the air.

CHAPTER FOUR

Murphy sat next to the bed with MJ in his lap. Brooke still hadn't opened her eyes. MJ squirmed until he stood. "I'm going to play with my marbles." He left the bedroom.

Murphy ran his hand over his face. He sure was tired. He'd kept vigil all night, and she'd hardly stirred. He couldn't quite figure it out. He hadn't seen any rocks she could have hit her head on. His breath had caught when he saw her go down. Quickly, he had pushed Nugget into the barn, closed the door, and then run to her.

At first he had been relieved. She'd had mud splattered all over her and he had almost laughed until he realized she was out cold. He'd swung her up into his arms. She weighed no more than she had on their wedding day.

When he got to the house, the door was open, and water was heating on the stove. MJ had grabbed all the towels he could find. Then he ran into Brooke's room and covered the bottom sheet with the towels.

"She'll have a fit if mud gets everywhere," he said seriously.

Murphy gave him a grateful nod and then he laid Brooke on her bed. He checked her head for any cuts or bruises but didn't see or feel any. Next, he took off her shoes and dress. He left the rest of her garments on.

"Here's the water, Murphy…" An angry expression came over the boy's face. "What are you doing? Ma is going to be upset. We need to cover her!"

"After I wash this mud off of her," he said calmly but firmly. "You can stay and make sure I'm not doing anything improper. I'm just tending to your ma is all."

MJ seemed to relax. "I'll stay."

Good young man, Murphy thought with approval, to be keeping an eye out for his ma like that. She had been raising him right.

Her neck and face were the worst. Murphy took the cloth and wet it in the warm water. Then he gently washed her face. Tenderness toward her overcame him, and he sighed. She looked just the same as the day they'd married. And his heart swelled with the same love he had felt back then. How was he going to convince her she was wrong about the whole situation? Somehow, he had to, for he knew he had never stopped loving her. He felt as fierce now as he had back then.

Next, he cleaned her neck, wrists, and hands. Her stockings were caked, but he didn't feel comfortable about taking them off. He scratched his head.

His eyes widened as MJ stepped forward and pulled them off from the toe. Well… that was one way to get it done.

"Do you think she's sleeping?" MJ's chin trembled.

"I think she will be just fine. She has us to watch over her."

"I'll pray for her. I bet that will help." MJ smiled.

"Never any harm in praying," Murphy encouraged with a smile as even more love flooded his heart, this for his son.

"Why don't you go and finish your supper? I'll stay right here."

MJ hesitated, but then with a resolute nod, he raced to the kitchen.

Brooke had mud in her hair, but they'd have to leave it for now. He had checked underneath the muddy mess to be sure she had no head wounds. He stepped back and studied her. There was nothing wrong with praying. In fact, his newest sister-in-law, Clarissa, was a mighty force now that she had complete faith in God. She had gone from being shy and thinking no one would want her to a confident mother-to-be. He smiled. He had never thought to see Donnell married. Donnell had always found fault with every woman he'd ever met. Murphy understood why he felt that way. Family secrets had been revealed and those had changed their entire family and their outlook on life. At least Clarissa had shown Donnell the way to God. It was almost a miracle the way Donnell smiled all the time now.

"Lord I've seen Your many miracles. I've always been grateful for Your presence in my life. Please help heal my wife. She's a stubborn one, and she doesn't believe in me, but I know she believes in You. Please lead us both to the truth. I keep asking myself the same question. Why did her father lie? Somehow, I need to prove the truth." He sighed. *"But one thing at a time. Please, Lord, heal Brooke. Amen."*

Murphy sat in the wooden chair next to her bed and took her hand in his. Had she thrown her wedding ring away? He always kept his in his pocket. Of course, he had thought her to be dead while she had believed he'd abandoned her. He shook his head to clear the rage that threatened. This wasn't the time for anger. If she didn't wake up soon, he'd ride to the nearest neighbor for help. He didn't want to leave Brooke and MJ alone that long, but he'd have no choice.

He brought her hand to his lips and kissed it. Her hands had fared better than he'd thought they would with all the plowing she'd done. There were a few places around her hard callouses that were raw. They'd heal, but he probably should wrap them. He stood and stared down on her. She still held his heart in those hands.

MJ helped him rip some old sheets into bandages. Then he handed Murphy a jar.

Murphy unscrewed the lid and took a cautious sniff, then cringed as his eyes watered. "What — Phew!"

"The worse it smells, the better it works." MJ nodded sagely.

"That's usually true. Let's go put some on her hands." Murphy allowed MJ to lead the way.

Murphy took off the lid again, and MJ held his nose closed. Unable to help himself, Murphy laughed. "I've smelled worse." Like horse manure covering a hole in a stable when he was hiding. He sat down and spread the ointment onto her hand, gently rubbing it in. Then he wrapped them with the cloth. She didn't react, not even so much as a whimper. Maybe she had a head wound he hadn't seen because of the mud. Washing her hair was going to be a messy job, but the mud was making her hair stiff.

"More hot water?" MJ asked.

Murphy nodded.

"I'll bring the soap too."

MJ was very intuitive. His son made him proud. One day soon he would claim MJ as his own.

He was right. Cleaning her hair left a huge wet mess by the time they were done. They were probably lucky that they hadn't drowned her. Every towel was mud-soaked as was the floor. Finally, he could better examine her head. There weren't any cuts, and he couldn't find a bump. Why wouldn't she wake up?

MJ jumped from one foot to the other and back again while he watched his mother. He was probably in a panic. Truth be told, Murphy was starting to panic too. He leaned over and stroked Brooke's cheek, murmuring to her, pleading with her to wake up. Then he kissed her on the lips, but she didn't kiss him back. So much for fairytales. He knew it wasn't good for a person with a head injury to sleep, but there wasn't anything he could do about it.

"My ma is sure to be mad that you kissed her." MJ stood with arms crossed over his chest, one eye narrowed. "One time there was this man in town and he grabbed her and kissed her and she walloped him."

Murphy smiled, he could imagine his feisty wife doing such a thing. "MJ, why don't you sit here while I try to clean the floors. Let me know if you see any movement at all." He allowed himself to grin. "And you're probably right. She probably will wallop me."

After throwing every dirty towel out into the yard, Murphy went back to the bedroom and turned around in a circle. "It's looking cleaner already."

"There is clean and then there is Ma clean. But I suppose this will do for now." MJ chuckled. "She hasn't moved at all. What do you suppose is the matter with her? I've fallen a bunch of times, and nothing like this ever happened."

It was hard to stare into eyes that were so much like his own. He wished he had an answer. MJ trembled now and then. He was probably trying to stay strong. He was a magnificent boy. Murphy shook his head sadly. He had no words to offer.

"Maybe I should be the one to kiss her?" suggested MJ. "She likes it when I kiss her on the nose and her cheeks and her chin. She says my kisses are magic kisses because they always make her feel better."

So much... he'd missed so so much. He didn't care what

anyone said. Even if he and Brooke never resolved their differences, he was staying to get to know his son. "I do believe you might be on to something."

MJ smiled and crawled up on the bed. He placed kisses all over his ma's face. He waited for a moment and then did it again.

Brooke shook her head. "Stop," she mumbled. "I'm trying to sleep."

Murphy lifted MJ off the bed and carried him out of the room. He gave MJ an enormous hug. "You did it! Your magic kisses saved your ma. Let's go make her something to eat while we let her rest for a bit longer."

MJ put his arms around Murphy's neck and buried his face in Murphy's shoulder. "I have to tell you a secret. I was scared. With Grandpa gone, I have a responsibility to the farm. I can do lots of stuff. My ma says I'm a big helper. This farm is going to be mine one day. I can't wait because I'm going to change it."

Murphy set him down. "Change it to what?"

"I'm not gonna plant anything. I'll keep the animals we have, but I have the best idea. I'm going to raise cats. Everyone loves cats. Right? You love cats too, don't you?" MJ stared up at him with his eyes wide.

Murphy hadn't really given it much thought. Cats were just cats, but there was no way he was going to disappoint MJ. "I like cats just fine. Do you have any yet?"

MJ nodded his head. "Our cat Blue just had a big litter of little cats. I've got my start already. I figure I could start out small and then by the time the farm is mine, I'll have enough cats for the whole place."

"You've really thought this out, haven't you?"

MJ's face brightened. "I've been planning it for some time now."

"It's always good to have a plan," Murphy told him. "After we feed your ma some lunch and make sure she's comfortable, let's go out to the barn to see Blue and her kittens."

"I don't call them kittens, I call them little cats."

Murphy's lips twitched. "I'll keep that in mind."

CHAPTER FIVE

It was finally nighttime, and MJ was in bed. Over twenty-four hours had passed since she'd been hurt, and Murphy sat by Brooke again. He'd missed her with everything inside him. There were times he questioned God why He had taken Brooke. And it was lies, all lies. If her father hadn't wanted her to leave the farm, all he'd had to do was ask. He hadn't needed to pull strings behind everyone's backs and cause an enormous mess. He hadn't needed to rob Murphy of his son.

Brooke murmured and sighed, but still didn't open her eyes. His wife was such a beautiful woman. Her skin was so soft and her lips were berry red. She hadn't cut her hair; it was longer than he remembered.

He longed for her smiles. They were his happiness. Life hadn't been happy while he'd thought her dead. It had been almost as if speaking about her death would make it all too real, unbearable. They hadn't gotten enough time together, but now... He wasn't leaving, and somehow, he had to convince her that he had not abandoned her.

"Your horse?" Brooke whispered hoarsely. "Did you get him into the barn?"

Startled out of his musings, he leaned toward her. "Yes, didn't put him in a stall, but got him out of the storm."

"How... how long...?"

"You've been out for a day," he answered quietly.

She gasped and tried to sit. "MJ!"

Murphy gave her a gentle push back to the pillow. "He's fine. He helped around the house and looked over you. I fed him, and now he's in bed."

She slumped back with a sigh. Then she tilted her head, listening. "It's still storming." Her brows furrowed as he became aware that the rain still drummed steadily on the roof.

"Yes, it's been raining on and off for a bit, but it's lighter now." Reaching out, he lightly patted her hand. She used to be frightened of storms. He remembered holding her tight until the storm blew over. From the worry on her face, he'd have to say she was still afraid.

Boldly, he stood and took off his boots and then climbed into bed with her, pulling her gently into his arms.

She stiffened but didn't struggle.

"It's just until the storm is over," he murmured. "I'm not trying to take advantage of the situation."

Her mouth opened as though she was going to say something, but there was a big loud boom of thunder, and she put her arms around his neck. She was holding him a little too tight to be comfortable, but he didn't say a word.

"You were very brave going to my campsite to get my belongings," he said, stroking her arm. "I never meant for you or MJ to be out in the storm. Thank you, though, for trying to save all my belongings. I treasure you and MJ much more than things, though. Besides, I always carry my most precious possession in my pocket."

She loosened her hold on his neck and looked him in the eye. "What is your most precious possession?"

He shoved his hand to his pants pocket and pulled out his wedding ring. "It's the only thing I had that you'd given me."

She stared at his open hand, her mouth opening and closing but no words emerging. When she spoke, her words were strained. "I'm not sure how I'm supposed to feel or how I'm supposed to act. I have been so furious and so hurt that I don't think I can let it all go. I can't say anything yet. I still don't have any proof that my father lied." Some tension drained from her body. "War changes people, and after I found out you were alive, I figured you decided you didn't want to be married anymore. It was so hard… grieving for you, especially when MJ was born. I looked forward to you coming home… meeting him… I was so proud I'd given you a son. I had always pictured us as a family, not a broken one. I—my father didn't tell me you were alive at first, but he finally had to, so I wouldn't go and look for another husband."

"Brooke…" he breathed, struggling against the emotions choking him. "I grieved too, and I didn't know about my son. You were the one thing that kept me going through the last years of the war. It was nothing but drudgery and killing, watching friends die… day in and day out. It took me well over a month to walk here just to find out you weren't here anymore. Your father didn't offer to let me stay. When I offered to help him, he told me to go. Heck, he seemed to begrudge the water I drank. I wanted to go into the house and touch our bed, but he wouldn't let me. I thought maybe I'd feel you in the bedroom. Stupid, I know."

Thunder crashed, and the entire house rattled. Brooke screamed, but Murphy put his lips over hers to quiet her. As soon as she calmed, he stopped kissing her. "I'm sorry about that. I just didn't want you to wake MJ. Is he afraid of storms too?"

She put her fingers to her lips, her eyes wide. "No, he's not. In fact, everyone thought it's funny that I am, especially him and my father. I couldn't act as though I wasn't afraid, so I usually sat in that corner over there with the quilt over my head shaking." She sighed loudly. "You haven't even asked if he is yours."

"I would never insult you that way. I have far too much respect for you. I know what we had; I know the love we shared. Plus, there's the fact he's the spitting image of me. A very handsome boy." He pulled her tight against him and kissed her forehead. "Why would you think I would ask?"

"There weren't many people who actually saw you. We got married here on the ranch, and I don't think you were ever in town. I didn't know anyone thought that way until I heard one prostitute, Bette, talking to another who worked at the saloon—I think her name is Adora. They laughed and thought it was convenient I had a ring on my finger since I was obviously pregnant." She snuggled against the shoulder. "I didn't go into town much after that. I've never been a social butterfly, so I missed nothing. Besides, if I needed anything Pa would always get it."

He rubbed his arm up and down her back. He'd longed for years to have her in his arms again. "What about church? They treated you with respect there, didn't they?"

There was a lengthy pause before Brooke said anything. "I haven't been to church since MJ was born. I just couldn't take it. I did nothing that I have any shame about, but there were always whispers and I didn't think it fair to subject my child to their lies. I had really thought I could rely on those women to help me when it was time for the baby to be born. I know there was a war on, and people didn't have much, but no one came with food. I always brought food to the other families when necessary. I knitted garments for their babies. I got nothing. The reverend never defended me, and he married us!"

Sadness filled him. He hadn't thought of how hard things must have been for her. "I'm so sorry that happened to you."

"I don't need your pity, I don't need anyone's pity," she snapped. "I am stronger than I ever was, and my relationship with God is deeper than ever before. There was one woman, Nelly, who drove out at the end of the war to tell me that my *supposed* husband was not on any of the death lists. I think she was looking for some type of reaction from me, but I just stared at her until she left." A shudder rippled through her. "I thought — I thought if you weren't on a death list then surely you were on your way back to me."

"I'm here now, and this will be an end to the gossip. My wife and child deserve to be treated with respect. I know you think little of me, but we spoke our vows before God, and to me those vows are binding." He squared his shoulders. "I think — I *know* we will have to make some sort arrangements for us both to live here. But I'm not leaving."

It had stopped storming, and Brooke pushed him away. "Well I'm not leaving either. Maybe we should build you a house of your own. Our maybe you can add a room to the barn. I'll leave that up to you. There will be one rule, and that rule is whatever I say to or about MJ is to stay that way. I don't want you getting in the middle if I need to send him to his room give him extra chores."

Murphy rolled out of bed and nodded. "It will take me a few days to scout out a spot for a house. I won't interfere with MJ, but I do want him to know his father."

She stiffened. "I'm not sure that's a good idea. What if you leave? I don't want you to break that little boy's heart." Tears filled her eyes.

"I'm not—" Frustration filled him, and he clenched his

jaw. There was nothing he could do or say that would change her mind. All he could do was to show her in action and words that he still loved her. He bent over and tucked the quilt around Brooke before he grabbed his boots. Then he walked to the door and turned. "I'll hold off. I promise you I will not hurt that child, my son." He quietly walked out the door and then drew it closed.

THE SUN WAS ALMOST TOO bright, and it gave her a headache. She'd have to ask MJ to gather the eggs later. Somehow, she must've hit her head; it hurt. And according to Murphy, she had lost an entire day. She rubbed her temple, glad she didn't have to face Murphy yet. Allowing him into her bed and letting him hold her was embarrassing. She never should've let it happen. It wasn't as though she was doing anything improper; after all, he was her husband. It was just the fact she'd been so mad at him for so long. Her feelings would not change overnight.

She went to the kitchen and cooked pancakes and bacon. She brewed plenty of coffee, knowing how Murphy liked coffee.

Her mind drifted, and she wondered what would have happened if Murphy had only come back to her at the end of the war...

They probably would have had more children. She'd always felt blessed she had MJ, but she also had a sense of bitterness because he was her only child.

Had her pa really sent Murphy away? It made no sense. What could he have been thinking? He knew how much she had loved Murphy. He knew MJ needed a father. He also knew how she had suffered with worry while the war had been going on. It was all too much to consider. True, her father had not been entirely honest about Murphy being dead, but he had confessed the truth later, that Murphy had just not come back for her. Her pa had wanted to spare her the heartbreak of feeling rejected and abandoned.

Part of her wanted to scream for Murphy to leave. To go back to his rich family and his big ranch. Forget her like he had before. But plain and simple, she could not work the farm alone. She was a hard worker and could do anything that needed done, but even her pa'd had hired help during their good years. As things stood, if it was just her working the land, they wouldn't have much of a crop. After flipping the last pancakes and allowing them to cook, she put them all in a big pile on a plate. She set the pancakes and bacon in the middle of the table. Then she stepped into the pantry and got one of her few jars of berry preserves. She placed that on the table too.

She sat and put her elbows on the table and then rested her face in her hands, keeping her eyes closed as the light gave her a headache. It had never seemed too bright in the kitchen before, but today it was for her. After a few minutes, she sat up straight and ran her fingers over her head. There, behind her left ear, she found a lump.

"Are you all right?" asked Murphy upon entering the house. "Maybe you should still be in bed."

She squinted at him. He was better looking than any man had a right to be. Even unshaven he was handsome. "I don't know, the light hurts my eyes. I found a lump behind my ear. I must have hit something when I fell."

Murphy walked to her and she lifted her hair so he could feel the lump.

"It's a good-sized one," he said, stepping back with a frown. "I'm surprised I missed it. I think it's back to bed for you."

"I kindly ask you not to tell me what to do. We will have

breakfast, I will clean up the kitchen, and then I'll probably go back to bed. Head injuries aren't usually things to ignore." She watched him for his reaction, but he didn't show one. Instead he helped himself to a cup of coffee and sat down at the table across from her.

MJ knocked on the door and Murphy hurried to open it. "Give me some of those." When they both turned, she could see that they each had more than enough eggs.

"Oh my, the hens certainly were laying. I'm surprised you managed to get them all back here. You did a splendid job, MJ."

MJ smiled. "I'm the man of the house since Grandpa died."

Brooke wasn't sure what to say, so she nodded and instructed them to put the eggs on the counter. "Breakfast is ready. Why don't we take our seats and say grace?"

"I want to say it this morning," MJ insisted.

That was just fine until he had trouble saying it. Murphy tried to help. MJ told him he could do it himself. Brooke frowned. Did her son not like Murphy? Did he think Murphy was stepping in his way? Maybe that was it. MJ was probably just marking his territory. It would work itself out. Besides, who really knew how long Murphy would stay?

For a few minutes, the clinking of silverware on plates filled the silence.

"Brooke, why aren't you eating?" Murphy asked after he swallowed a mouthful of pancakes. "I know your eyes hurt, but are you feeling all right other than that? You still look slightly pale. Can I get you something else to eat?"

She shook her head, then cringed; the pain was back. She closed them, hoping for the pain to ebb. MJ was out of his chair in a flash and stood by her side.

"Ma, Murphy is right you don't look good." He hastened

to add, "Not that you look ugly or anything. It's more of a not-so-good look. I can do the dishes."

Brooke's eyes filled with tears. "You are the sweetest boy." She took his hand, held it and closed her eyes again. The scraping sound of the chair moving didn't surprise her. Murphy would want to have his say.

He scooped her up and she let go of MJ's hand. Whatever happened to asking a person if she wanted to go to her room right then? She been running her own life for a very long time, although she did once have her father's help. But now, decisions she made for herself and MJ were *her* decisions. Murphy set her onto the bed so she was sitting. He even plumped up her pillows and put them behind her back.

"Is there anything I can bring you?" he asked.

MJ bounded into the room, a bundle of energy. "Ma, I'll bring you a cup of water and your sewing. I can also find a book for you to read. Is there anything else you need?"

"All of that sounds wonderful to me, MJ, thank you." She waited for MJ to leave and then she looked up at Murphy. "I'm not sure why, but I think MJ is trying to compete with you. You need to figure out a way for him to still have the responsibility of keeping me safe while you're here. My father told him many times 'no matter what, make sure your ma is safe.'"

Murphy's brows rose. Then he nodded as if he'd found the answer to a long hard puzzle. "I was wondering. Don't worry, things will be set to rights. I can see the bond you two have. I can't deny that I'm jealous of your relationship, but I have all the patience in the world. I don't want you to worry about it." He put his hand on her shoulder and gave it a quick squeeze before he moved away from the bed.

MJ's arms were full as he joined them. Brooke took the water from him and smiled.

"I got your sewing. Looks like you're trying to patch

another pair of my pants." He put the basket and the pants on the bed, and then he took the Bible out of the basket and set it in her lap. "I know this is your favorite book."

Her heart swelled to near bursting. "I don't know what I would do without you, MJ. You know everything I like and everything I need. Now I need some time alone as my eyes hurt. I just want to lie here with them closed and perhaps I might be a lady of leisure and take a nap." She opened her arms and waited for him to step into them and then gave him an enormous hug.

He pulled away with a grin, then walked to the bedroom door. "Come on, Murphy, we have chores to do. There's no lollygagging on this farm. If you want to eat, you need to work." MJ walked out of the room as though he expected Murphy to follow right behind.

Murphy smiled, and then he bent down and kissed her cheek. "You rest. I'll do enough work for both of us so we can all eat tonight."

She couldn't help herself, she chuckled as she watched him leave. Yes, his shoulders were wider, but she didn't have time to think about that now her head really hurt.

CHAPTER SIX

*M*urphy enjoyed himself while allowing MJ to order him around. His son sure did know a lot about farming. The sun had been out for half the day, and now it was pouring once again. They were in the barn and he heard a horse approaching. He stepped out into the rain and it was a woman riding on a paint. He quickly lifted her down, almost knocking off the ridiculous hat she wore. He was never one for feathers and other froufrous on hats.

The woman's eyes widened as she stared at Murphy. "I don't know where Brooke found you, but I hope there's more." She laughed. "Come on, MJ, let's get out of this rain." She swiftly walked across the yard and went into the house. Murphy shook his head. Who was that?

Her horse was soaking wet, so he took him in and got him settled. As soon as he was done, he made a run for it back to the house. He immediately took off his boots and was surprised to see MJ and the woman playing checkers.

She stood and offered a smile. "I'm Robin Macy. The Malerys and I have been friends forever. And you are?"

Murphy gave her a nod as he put his wet hat on the table

next to the door. "It's very nice to meet you, Miss Macy. I'm Murphy Kavanagh." He could tell she wanted to ask him a lot of questions, but he walked into the kitchen, taking away her opportunity. "Can I get you some coffee or tea?" he called from the kitchen.

"Thank you," Miss Macy answered. "Some tea would be lovely."

Tea, huh? He could make tea. How hard could it be? He'd had tea before. He looked all over the kitchen and finally found a jar with tea leaves. He threw a couple handfuls into the bottom of his clean coffee pot and topped it off with water. All he needed to do now is let it boil for a while until it was done. He got down one of the two teacups with saucers and set it on a tray. Were there any cookies to put with it? He didn't spot any. What did one put on the tray when there weren't cookies? She'd just have to make do with tea. He waited and waited until it boiled a good long time. He poured the tea into the cup and carried the tray into the other room.

"The tea took me a bit longer to make and I apologize for the delay. I don't make tea often, but when I do people seem to like it." He took the saucer with the cup of tea and set it on the table in front of Miss Macy. "There's nothing like a good warm drink on such a rainy day."

He watched her and waited, but she hadn't sipped her tea. Maybe she was letting it cool off. "So what brings you to the farm?"

"I came to make sure that Brooke was being properly taken care of. I'm not happy that the light gives her such a headache."

Murphy was stunned. "How did you know?"

MJ jumped up and down next to his chair. "Robin always knows when someone needs some doctorin'."

Miss Macy stared at the cup of tea and took a sip. She set

the cup back down on the saucer and gave Murphy an amused smile. "I do appreciate the effort you made on my behalf, Mr. Kavanagh but I'm afraid you boiled bay leaves instead of tea." Her lips twitched and she put her hand in front of her mouth as if trying to hide a smile.

"So, I shouldn't pour a cup for Brooke?" He offered a simple grin.

"Oh dear, no. But if you let me into the kitchen, I brought my own blend of tea that should help."

Murphy quickly stood. "The kitchen is that way." He pointed, hoping she would hurry and make the tea for Brooke.

"Yes, I know where the kitchen is, but thank you. MJ, why don't you give me a hand while Murphy goes upstairs and lets Brooke know I'm here."

MJ hurried into the kitchen; he must like Miss Macy. Murphy went up the stairs and peeked into Brooke's room. She sat there on the bed with her eyes closed, a look of pain on her face, and he hoped Miss Macy and her tea would help.

He walked in and waited near the door. He didn't want to disturb Brooke, but he wasn't sure that she was actually sleeping.

"Why aren't you wearing your boots?"

Well, there was his answer. Murphy took a couple steps closer to her. "They're wet and muddy so I left them by the front door. You have a visitor. She's making you some tea right now."

Brooke smiled. "I was hoping she would come. I need to keep more of her teas and herbs in the house. She's wonderful, isn't she? She seems to know and always comes when needed. I don't know how she does it, but I'm glad she does. Is MJ with her? He loves to watch her, and he asks her all kinds of questions. She has so much patience she answers them all."

"Did you want me to carry you downstairs or did you want to stay here?"

"Staying here would probably be best. I can't wait to drink her tea and have my head stop pounding. How did you and MJ get on?"

Murphy gave her smile. "He's a born leader. He knew what needed to be done and how to do it. You have every reason to be proud of that boy. Plus, I was told I was an outstanding worker. Made my day."

Brooke started to laugh, then winced. "That hurts." She touched her head.

"There you are," Robin said cheerfully. She gave Murphy a speculative look. "I brought my tea for you."

"Well if you ladies are all set, I'll find something for MJ and I to do." His gaze lingered on Brooke before he turned and left.

Robin stared at Brooke. "That isn't... Could that be?"

Brooke's eyes filled as she nodded.

Robin handed Brooke a cup of the willow bark tea. "Tell me."

Brooke sipped her tea. Where to start? "You're the only one who knows my husband is alive. There were some papers that needed to be signed after my father's death. The lawyer never said a word to me about Murphy. He just asked me to come to a meeting. It startled me to see him there. And I think it startled him even more. The lawyer explained how the farm now belonged to Murphy." She took another sip of tea. "I figured I'd need to pack and leave. I thought that would be the end, but it wasn't. He camped right at the edge of the property, and of course he saw MJ."

"What was his excuse for never coming back? He left you all alone. What kind of man does that?"

Brooke shrugged her right shoulder. "He has some farfetched story about how my father told him I was dead. Murphy said that he came here when the war was over. He says my father showed him a grave and told him it was me."

"What were you supposed to have died of? Where is the supposed grave?"

"There's a large rock next to my mom's grave, and Murphy said my father claimed that was my marker. Murphy told me he offered to stay and help my father with the farm, but he was told to leave. It just doesn't sound like my father. I mean yes, he did lie to me about Murphy being alive at first, but he was trying to protect me." She squeezed her hands into fists as a wave of despair threatened to drown her. "Robin… What kind of man doesn't come to his wife after a war but goes to his family home instead? I mourned him for so long, but I decided to look for another husband. That's when my Pa finally told me Murphy was alive, he just never came home to me. He thought it would take some of the pain away, but it made it worse."

Robin settled one hand on Brooke's forearm. "Listen, I know you're hurting. I've seen it in your eyes, it must have been unbearable to know your husband was living elsewhere. It certainly wasn't fair you not being able to remarry. I remember how excited you were when you had MJ and you couldn't wait for Murphy to come home. Maybe you and Murphy need to talk."

"Robin, we have talked. My heart is telling me that the only reason he is here is for MJ. I need to protect my son. Who knows if Murphy will stick around or not? And personally, I can't take much more disappointment. I'm still grieving for my father."

Robin slid her palm along Brooke's arm and took her hand. "What way does Murphy look at you?"

"He looks at me like I'm crazy. He thinks I'm supposed to believe everything he says." Brooke huffed out a breath. "And he's doing a lot of work around here. I'm not the same girl he married, not by a longshot. I'm independent, and I can take care of myself. I don't need a man around here. I've raised my son without a father so if he wants to go he can go."

"Has he mentioned leaving?" Robin poured more tea.

"No, in fact he seems to think he's staying. I can't order him off his property. Especially since it was legally his. When he told me he was staying, I bravely gave him two options. Build himself another house or build himself a room off the barn. It didn't seem to faze him. I look at him, and I remember how sweet and gentle he was. I remember loving him with everything inside me, but now that love has been replaced with bitterness. If I push... I'm afraid he might just take MJ and leave."

"I don't know, he didn't seem the type of man to do that, but you know him better than I." She tilted her head to the side. "Would it be so bad if he stayed so MJ could have a father?"

"I told him not to tell MJ who he is. I'm terrified my son will get hurt. That is... we'll tell him, eventually. MJ has the right to know." She drank more of the tea. "What are the people in town saying?"

"Most believe he is your long-lost husband. Then there are a few who think you're a hussy, but you know I wouldn't worry about it. Why don't you take this time to get to know him again?" Robin smiled at her. "I need to get back. Is there anything else you need before I go?"

"Thank you for being such a wonderful friend and thank you for the tea. One way or the other, I'll be fine. This farm belongs to me, not to my husband. I don't care what a piece of paper says. I guess I'll just wait and see how long it takes for him to leave."

Robin took the cup from Brooke and set it on the side table. "Take it easy for a few days just in case. You got a lot going on in that head of yours. You take care now."

Brooke watched as Robin left, and then her thoughts drifted to Murphy. Would he stay? She sighed. Probably not. If he could help her get the crops planted that would be wonderful. He could leave right after that. She gave a slight headshake. She'd be lucky if he stayed that long.

Her heart fluttered when she thought of MJ. There was an obvious bond between father and son. MJ deserved his attention; she just hoped it didn't lead to heartache. She squeezed her eyes shut, so tired her brain felt jumbled. What if her father *had* lied? It felt like a betrayal to even think that way. He'd been so good to MJ, taking to him like he was his own son rather than his grandson. Her eyelids drifted downward.

THE BOUNCING of her bed woke her. She felt groggy and seeing the light still hurt a bit, but it was better than before. She smiled at MJ. "What have you two been doing?"

MJ stopped bouncing and handed her a small bouquet of wildflowers. "This is from both of us. Me and Murphy. Murphy said women like flowers. Do you like them, Ma? Do you?"

She shifted her gaze, and Murphy smiled at her. It was an authentic smile. She had expected a mocking smile. She looked into her son's eyes and cupped his face. "They are the finest flowers I have ever been given. Thank you so much for thinking of me."

"Murphy said it'd be like bringing some sunshine indoors

for you. Do you think that's how it is?" MJ's eyes grew wide waiting for her answer.

"It sure feels that way. Thank you both for your thoughtfulness." She looked at Murphy. "Do you think you could handle supper for tonight? It doesn't have to be anything fancy. Maybe you should cook some eggs since we have so many of those. Thank you for watching MJ."

He gave her a lazy smile, the smile he knew she couldn't resist. "I'd do anything for you."

Brooke quickly looked away. "MJ, do you think you could show Murphy where everything is in the kitchen? It will be an enormous help."

MJ jumped up and ran out of the room saying, "Yes, ma'am."

"How are you feeling? Does your head still hurt?" He moved until he was right next to the bed. His nearness made her heart flutter.

"I feel better knowing MJ is enjoying his time with you. I still have a little headache, but I'm sure it will be better. If you need to leave, I could always have you go get Robin. She can stay here." She met his gaze and realized he was staring.

"I don't have plans to leave." He shook his head. "However, I have to go to town eventually to let my family know I'll be staying here for a while. I can't wait until they learn about you and MJ."

Her mouth opened, and then she frowned. "They don't know you got married? You're ashamed of me, aren't you? You would've told them if you thought I was really dead. You didn't tell them because you didn't want to come back here and you didn't want their judgment. I'd like to be left alone for a while." She turned her head. She wanted nothing to do with him anymore. He was a low-down snake for sure.

She heard him leave, and that was a relief. She'd almost fallen for his story full of his lies. Somehow, he'd become her weakness, and she couldn't have that. You needed to be strong and had to be smart to keep your land and survive. There wasn't room for him, not anymore.

She glanced down at the flowers she still grasped in her hand. It was sad to say, but they were the first flowers she'd ever received. Her heart tugged. They sure were beautiful. So she would just consider them from MJ and not from Murphy.

CHAPTER SEVEN

MJ had insisted Murphy sleep in his grandpa's room. Brooke wished she could protest, but MJ was so excited. It had been a week now, and it hadn't been as annoying as she'd thought it would be. Murphy was a hard worker, and he gave her a lot of time to herself. She had time for planting her garden, picking berries and canning. They ate meals together, though, and there was no denying MJ was thriving under Murphy's attention.

Murphy watched her almost all the time. Every time she turned and caught him, he'd quickly look away. There was always plenty of wistfulness in his eyes. Every day she expected him to leave. Would he say goodbye or just sneak off? He'd been kind, kinder than she'd been, but she couldn't forget he had lived on his ranch all this time. Why hadn't he told his family about her if he thought her dead? That was what family was for, to help a person get through the hard times.

The wood Murphy ordered for his house had been delivered yesterday. He didn't say a word about it to her. He'd shown MJ the plans. They talked about it plenty. Her heart hurt and the feeling of being left out was always there. It was as though he was making a statement that he didn't care what she thought, he could do what he wanted.

Bread needed to be made, but going to her parents' graves was more important. She wandered to the gigantic tree. She loved the smell of freshly turned soil. Closer to the graves, she smelled the sweet scent of flowers.

Her steps faltered and then she halted in her tracks. Flowers lay at both graves, and shoots pushed through the earth with a promise of planted flowers. There wasn't even a weed to pull. She sat on the ground between the graves. Even though she was an adult with a child, there were times she felt the need for advice or a hug from her ma and pa.

"Pa, I just can't allow myself to believe his story. I've had too many lonely years. And if Murphy thought me to be dead, why didn't he remarry? The land is mine, and one way or the other I'm getting a signed deed." She sighed. "MJ is wonderful. He works hard and is ever learning. And his daddy... Well, he is still a handsome devil, especially with that grin of his." She dropped her chin down to her chest. Heat covered her face. "I just don't know what to do. We could have been happy at one time but now... I don't know if we'll ever close the gap between us. He lied to me."

Usually she felt better after visiting her folks, but not today. She stood next to their graves on the hill and surveyed the surrounding property. It was large enough to run a couple hundred head of cattle. Would that be possible? Would it be the best course of action? Taking a deep breath, she shook her head. How much land she had would depend on where Murphy built his house.

And speaking of handsome devils... She groaned. Murphy was striding her way. What lies did he have to tell today?

"MJ put those flowers on your parents' graves," he said

before she could greet him. "He told me you planted bulbs on your Ma's grave last fall. I didn't expect to see anything growing for a few more weeks."

"Did you tell him you thought my pa to be a liar?" she shot at him. " What have you told him about where you've been? I'm confident you came up with an impressive story for him."

She winced for a second at the hurt on his face.

"I most certainly did not tell him one thing about your pa," Murphy said in a level voice. "It's plain as day he loves his grandpa and that his grandpa loved him. As for me, the only 'story' I have is the true one. I was told and believed that you were dead. And I haven't told him all about that one because I don't know the complete story." He kicked a rock. "You know, every day I work this farm hoping you will see that I intend to stay. I keep thinking, 'today she'll learn to trust me,' but that never happens. I saw the look on your face when MJ and I were going over the house plans. You could have joined us, but you intentionally keep yourself apart." He stalked a few feet away, but then turned and came back, sadness in his features. "I'm wondering what happened to that sweet joyful woman I married. I don't mean that you're a shrew, but you used to smile all the time. I've missed those smiles. I know my being here has been a big shock to you but think about how I felt at the lawyer's office when I saw you. It was a shock seein' the woman I thought was dead standin' there. I mourned you, and now I'm mourning you again. I feel like I lost you twice. Honestly, I don't know where to go from here. I intend to raise my son. Now, I'm not sure how you think this is all going to work. Will he sleep at my house and eat at yours?"

She gasped and stared at him for a minute. The sadness on his face had changed to anger. Well, she was angry too. Angry that he had left her, angry that when he came back, he came with a passel of lies. "Don't you dare put this on me. I've been the one who has been here every single day of that child's life. I'm the one who went without sleep worrying every time he had a sniffle. Pa would just tell me not to worry about it, but I am that boy's mama, and mamas worry. I really didn't have anyone to lean on and that hurt. How I wished and wished that you were here, but you were on your ranch instead."

His face turned dark crimson. "Don't you think it hurts me I've missed so much? Do you really believe I would turn my back on my own son? Did you really think my love was so shallow I'd walk away? Every time I look at you, I want to gather you up in my arms and kiss you senseless, but I don't. I know my attentions wouldn't be welcome. Do you really think your pa is the type of man who would *allow* your husband to just walk away? Because I think he was the kind of man who would have ridden out and brought me back here no matter what it took."

Brooke opened her mouth to respond, but no words came. Was Murphy right? Her pa had always tried to give her everything she wanted from the time she was small. He'd even run off the Dewberry boy for taunting her about not knowing how to ride a horse when she was six and then spent the next week teaching her how to ride.

Murphy drew a deep breath, and when he spoke again, he seemed to have his fury in control. "I do thank you for the time you give me with MJ. You've done a wonderful job raising him. Somehow, we need to appear as though we like each other for MJ's sake." He rubbed the back of his neck. "Oh, and I'm not building a new house. I'm adding on to the one we have. I'm also replacing some wood that's gone rotten. I would've told you all about it if you had just asked instead of giving me your perpetual frown. I've got work to do." He turned and walked away without looking back.

Now she too knew what it felt like to lose the same person twice. She'd never dated before she'd married. She wasn't schooled in the ways of men and women. She didn't know how to act around her own husband. He was a hardheaded man and adding onto the house was not one of the options she had given him. But she'd try to get along and act happy for MJ's sake.

Slowly, she ambled to the house, not feeling like doing much at all. She wanted to sit and contemplate some of the things Murphy had said to her. But there was always something that needed to be done on the farm. Right now, she needed to make bread.

MURPHY PUSHED HIS HAT, so it sat back farther on his head. He'd never understand women. Why she couldn't accept the truth was beyond him. He was the one who'd been wronged. He was the one who had been lied to. He was the one who had been kept from his son. He was the one who'd missed her with everything he had. Why? Why had her father gone to such extremes to keep them apart? Did he think his daughter deserved better? They hadn't always seen eye to eye, but he had never been left with the impression that her father hated him to that degree.

Every day, Brooke made it clear that she was suffering through Murphy's presence for the sake of their son. Every day, no matter how he tried or what he did, she made it clear it was not enough, never would be enough. And that she thought he was lying.

Could he live on this farm knowing that Brooke hated him? He wasn't sure he could do that, but for MJ's sake he had to try it. If it didn't work, he would buy the land next to the farm and raise cattle. There was no way he would leave

MJ. In his dreams, Brooke was always smiling at him with love in her eyes. So very different from how she looked at him now. At least she hadn't put up a fuss about him enlarging the house. He planned to make a master bedroom and an office.

Watching MJ play with his cat Blue, Murphy smiled. How were the "little cats" doing? He'd have to remember to ask later. The frustration he felt about his relationship with Brooke was minor compared to the love he had for his son. Maybe someday he would have more children with Brooke. He almost laughed at his last thought. *That* probably would not happen.

"Murphy, how long do you think it takes for little cats to become big cats?" asked MJ, looking up. "Do you think I should get more big cats so they can make more little cats? What about naming them? You think I should name the little cats? I mean, there's a lot of them. What did Mama say when you told her about my idea?"

Murphy looked down and smiled. "You know your ma's been feeling a bit left out. We need to share our ideas with her. I think she would be better suited to answering your little cat, big cat questions."

MJ closed his eyes and shook his head back and forth. "It's all my fault. I'm supposed to take care of Ma. I didn't know she was feeling left out. It's not a good feeling, Murphy. I need to be more sensitive, but girls are hard to figure."

Murphy laughed. "They certainly are hard to figure."

That night Brooke tossed and turned. Finally, she slipped out of bed and went to the window. The moon was glowing. At her wedding, she had spoken vows before God. She was married to Murphy "until death do they part." That could be a very long time. She had at one time wanted more children. But now... it did not seem likely that MJ would have any brothers or sisters.

Lord, I need Your help. I've always trusted my father, and he never steered me wrong. But I've never known Murphy to lie either. I felt like such a fool when I learned that Murphy never came back for me, and I can't shake the feeling. Please open my heart so I can see the truth. And Lord protect MJ through this. Sometimes adults seem to make a mess of everything. Amen.

Despite her faith, praying didn't give her the relief she expected. God would only do so much, and the rest was up to her. She would end up having to forgive someone, her father or Murphy. God would help her and guide her. She would need as much help as He would give her.

The shadows were long, and she watched as they changed with the wind. When they had talked before they got married, Murphy had said he was fine living on the farm. Now she wasn't so sure. She worried her lip. She leaned forward, thinking she saw something, but then nothing was there. She stood there, not moving except to take a step back. She watched and watched and her patience paid off. There was a man out there trying to get into the barn. Terror filled her as she ran to Murphy's room.

He was a light sleeper she had barely walked into his room before he opened his eyes and instantly set up. "What is it? What's wrong?"

"Grab your guns there's somebody outside trying to get into the barn. I grabbed the rifle over the mantel." She turned and took off at a run.

"You stay here. I'll go outside."

"Don't fight me on this, Murphy. I am going," she whispered before she opened the front door.

Once outside, Murphy immediately took the lead. The

barn door was open and blowing in the wind. He peered inside but saw nothing. "You stay here I'll be right back."

She was right behind Murphy as he entered the barn. She could tell by the stiffening of his neck he knew she didn't obey him. Maybe he didn't know how handy she was with a rifle. The door slammed, and the loud noise made her jump.

Murphy put his finger to his nose, indicating they needed to be quiet. He inched toward the door and tried to open it. He put his gun back into his holster and tried to open it with both hands.

"Are we locked in?" she whispered.

"It sure seems that way." Murphy frowned as he cast his gaze around the barn. He took his pistol back out and then he checked each stall. "We're alone in here."

She shook her head. "I don't understand what's going on? Why would someone do this? Oh no, what about MJ?" Her heart thumped madly against her chest. Her little boy was in the house alone. "Don't just stand there do something," she hissed.

"I'm thinking." He looked as though he was trying to hold his anger inside. He went to each wall and pushed and then, kicked. "Who built this thing? I've never seen a barn so sturdy."

They both turn their heads at the sound of a horse racing by. Brooke thought she was going to be sick. Bile rose into her throat. She swallowed it back down; getting sick wouldn't help. "It looks like we either dig under the barn or we climb up to the hayloft, push as much hay as we can to the ground and then jump."

"Both are worthy ideas but I think I have one that will be easier." He took a long coil of rope hanging on the barn wall. Then he climbed up into the hayloft, tying one end of the rope to the beam closest to the opening of the barn. He threw the rope down and nodded. "It reaches the ground. I will climb down and then open the door for you."

Wide-eyed, she nodded. What if he fell? She didn't have a good feeling about this whole thing. She barely could see him leap away from the opening, and it was less than a minute before he opened the door. He took her hand and they ran to the house. Once again, he was in the lead as they went in.

Her heart seemed to stop when she peered into MJ's room. His bed was empty, and his covers were on the floor in a pile. She put her hand to her chest and tried to take deep breaths as she walked into the room and looked all around. She glanced up and she knew the fright she saw in Murphy's eyes probably mirrored her own.

"Why would anyone take MJ? I will search the rest of the house." She frantically ran from room to room until she got to the room that was her father's the one that Murphy was now using. The furniture had been moved.

"Looks like they were looking for something."

Her hands trembled. "They?"

He pulled her back against him. "I shouldn't have said they. I see no sign there was more than one. What in tarnation could someone be looking for?"

She walked forward out of Murphy's embrace and sank onto the end of the bed, shaking her head. She looked all around trying to identify if there was anything else out of place, but she didn't know what she was looking for. "I do not understand. Did my father have something hidden?" Despair overcame her, and a sob slipped out. "Oh, Murphy, we need to get MJ back. I need my little boy, my baby home with me." Tears streamed down her face.

Murphy laid a hand on her shoulder. "We will find him."

Brooke quickly wiped her tears away and stood up. "I need to get dressed, and we'll need supplies. I'm hoping we can track whoever took MJ."

"I'll meet you out front with the horses saddled."

She slowly nodded and then he left. Was she dreaming? This had to be a horrible nightmare. *This can't be happening.* She looked around the room again, but there was nothing. Taking a deep breath, she let it out and raced to get dressed. Her hands shook, but she was finally ready.

Please Lord, help us find MJ.

"I found their trail," Murphy said grimly, stepping through the door. "We can walk the horses until the sun is up."

"Murphy, we need to ride and get MJ back as quickly as possible." Her heart hurt more and more, and her sense of panic wanted to take over.

"We need to do it the right way, the safe way." Murphy reached out and entwined his fingers with hers. He held the reins for both horses, and they walked. He comforted her by holding her hand. Together they could do this. But he was right. They needed to keep their wits about them.

Dawn was upon them finally. It seemed like an eternity waiting for the sun to show. Murphy helped her mount her horse.

"Are those britches you're wearing under your dress?" He shook his head.

Brooke stiffened. "You disapprove?"

He mounted up on his horse. "No, I think it's smart." He took the lead, following the trail.

THE KIDNAPPER DIDN'T HIDE his tracks. They were headed south of town. Was he leading them to his house? Murphy could tell they weren't very far ahead. He stopped and twisted to look at Brooke. "You sure you don't know who took him?"

"No, but the Dooley family lives close. Guy Dooley wanted to marry me, but he wouldn't…" Her eyes widened.

"Ready your gun, they aren't far."

She gave him a quick nod, and he turned back around. He needed to be sure MJ didn't get hurt. Between the trees, he saw a house. He jumped down and then helped Brooke down. They left the horses behind as they crept toward the house. He had his rifle and plenty of ammunition.

MJ's voice could be heard asking all kinds of questions. It was good to know he hadn't been harmed, and he didn't seem scared. They drew closer, and Murphy saw a young man with long stringy hair sitting on one of the steps to the house. He sure looked glum. Before he knew it, Brooke took the lead.

She stepped into the yard and stalked toward the house. "Guy, what do you think you're doing? Why would you take MJ? Do you have any idea how upset I've been?" She kneeled, and MJ ran into her arms.

"I see you brought your new man," said Guy in a bitter voice. "You were promised to me! Your pa and I made a fair trade, but he never paid up. He was supposed to see that we married. Now you have some man living with you. It don't look good, Brooke."

"What did you give my father?"

"A map to a gold mine. I won it in a card game." Guy lifted his chin.

Murphy took a step toward Guy, but stopped when the other man tensed. "Have either of you ever seen the mine?"

Guy stood and straightened his shoulders. "No, but it was put in the pot as being worth twenty dollars."

"Guy, there probably isn't a mine."

"Don't care." He shrugged. "I was promised Brooke by her pa, and I plan to collect. I knew she'd come after her son."

"She can't marry you," Murphy bit out. "She's already married to me. Sorry, but her father lied to you."

Guy threw his hat on the ground. "I don't believe you! You two haven't gone into town together, and the preacher ain't been at your place!"

Murphy's stomach churned that the man knew so much about them.

"You've been watching us?" Brooke stood, anger and disgust etched into her expression. "I don't care what you thought! How dare you steal my child! What was your plan if I refused to marry you? What if we didn't see your trail and never ended up at your house?" She pushed MJ behind her and leaned forward, her lips curled into a snarl. "You stay away from me, you hear me?"

Guy's neck turned crimson and then his face became the same color. "I want the map!"

Murphy growled. "You didn't copy it before you gave it to her father?"

Guy stared at the ground. "I didn't think of that. I didn't find it in your house."

Brooke shook her head. "No, and you won't because I don't believe there is a map. But you left me a monumental mess to clean!" She lifted her hand and pointed a finger at Guy. "I meant it. You stay away."

The screen door opened, and an elderly woman stepped out, her face twisted in rage. She grabbed Guy's ear. "Out causing trouble, were you? I will whoop you again."

Guy cried out in pain as she dragged him into the house.

After only a moment, the woman stepped back outside. "I'm so sorry he made trouble for you, Brooke. Guy doesn't use the brain God gave him. If you don't report him to the sheriff, I'd be obliged." The woman looked to be on the verge of a breakdown. "I'll see to it he stays away from you and yours."

Brooke walked to the woman and took her hand. "There is no need to worry about that. Guy made a poor trade with my father."

Her eyes glittered. "What was the trade?"

"Me for a treasure map."

Mrs. Dooley shook her head. "A terrible trade indeed. Everyone's been waiting for your husband to finally come to his senses and come back for you." She opened the door and walked inside.

Brooke put her hands on her hips and stared at the house. "When you didn't come back, my pa told everyone my husband had died in the war." She narrowed her eyes. "I wonder who else knew you were alive…"

Aside from his whole family? Murphy shrugged. "I have no idea. MJ, do you want to ride with me?"

"Yes, Murphy!" MJ raced to the waiting horses.

CHAPTER EIGHT

The lump in her throat had been stuck there ever since she had seen Mrs. Dooley. Murphy seemed to take it all in stride and thank goodness MJ didn't ask questions. What was she supposed to do? Did she even have a choice? Everyone seemed to know her husband had finally come back.

UGH!

They'd need to talk to MJ before… He might have heard what she and Murphy had said to Guy Dooley as it was. He might be peppering Murphy with questions at that moment. Her entire body tensed. She should go find them. But her feet seemed unable to carry her as a sense of doubt flooded her heart.

Maybe she should have gone after Murphy when she found out he was alive. She should have demanded he help raise MJ or help with the farm. Shame had kept her away. He'd left them, rejected her and gone on living the life he'd had before the war.

She'd loved him with her whole heart. He had meant everything to her and when she thought him dead; she wanted to die too, but she had MJ who needed her. If Murphy had cared even a tiny bit, he would have checked on her. When her father told her Murphy was really alive and he just never came home to her, she had built a wall around her heart. Only MJ could get in.

She hadn't realized it was happening, but the walls had been slowly coming down. No, she needed to build them back up again or she would be hurt.

She thought again of Guy's mother telling her everyone had been waiting for Murphy to come back. Her pa had been courting the Widow Dooley. Perhaps that was how she'd known. Maybe no one else knew. Brooke suppressed a groan. Mrs. Dooley wasn't known for her discretion.

She worried her lip until it bled. All she wanted was to run and run. But a mother couldn't do that. She put her finger to her mouth, and her lip wasn't bleeding anymore. But there was still so much emotion roiling inside her, and she finally acknowledged it as rage. But with the rage came a sense of clarity. Murphy'd had no reason to lie. And he had appeared shocked when she had walked into Tom Faber's office. He'd been shaken, not expecting to see her. All at once she realized her father must have lied to both her and Murphy. It was the only explanation for why he was saying he'd thought her dead.

Why? What could have driven him to ruin her life and take away her chance at happiness? She walked toward the kitchen and spotted the mess in his room. She needed to put that to rights. It helped, pushing the furniture back to where it belonged. *I'll never know why Pa betrayed me like that.* Hearing a noise, she glanced up and Murphy stood in the doorway watching her. The pain and the betrayal in his eyes were there for her to see. Instead of welcoming him home, she'd tried to get him to leave.

With a cry of anguish, she flew into his arms and sobbed

against his chest. She cried about her father's lies. She cried for the long lonely nights. She cried for the other children they should have had, and she cried because he'd thought her dead. So much wasted time. MJ would have had a father almost from the beginning. Forgiveness wouldn't come easy, but she'd work on it. It had been up to God to decide who should be forgiven, and now she realized she needed to forgive herself first, because she had hardened her heart against her husband.

Murphy held her tight and rocked her back and forth as she sobbed. Then she saw MJ watching them, and she pulled away. "I need to tell MJ."

Murphy drew her back into his arms. "I just told him."

Her heart stopped as her world tilted. "You told him?

"He's happy about it."

It was understandable MJ was happy. Now he had a pa to show to his friends and a good man to look up to. But she had wanted to be the one to tell him, and she had to stem a sense of disappointment.

"My father lied about everything," she admitted. She felt broken, and she hadn't a clue how to put herself back together.

"I know, and we'll talk about it later tonight. You must be reeling." He drew away and gazed at her face, and then he leaned forward and kissed her cheek.

She left the warmth of his arms in search of her son. MJ was her primary concern. She sat on the sofa and pulled him up next to her. "Is there anything you wanted to ask me? You must have questions."

His eyes were wide, and his expression was serious. "I'm glad I have a pa. Why aren't you happy, Mama? Pa was gone a long time, but he told me he's here to stay. Could you try to be nice to him?"

His hopeful look would be her undoing one of these days.

"Yes, I will be nice to your father. I want you to be happy." Part of her warned that she shouldn't make promises she might not be able to keep. It was all too new.

"It's not hard to be nice. He's not grouchy like Grandpa was." MJ nodded his head.

She glanced at Murphy. "You have a point. He's not grouchy. He has nice manners too."

"He's fun, and he likes me. I look just like him." MJ puffed out his chest.

"Yes, you have from the minute you were born. I always thought you looked like your father." She heaved a sigh. "We have to have a few rules."

"Awww."

"Your pa is not a toy or a dog to play with. You are to listen to him. He's a good man who will do everything he can to keep you safe." She glanced at Murphy and found him grinning at her. "If I have already told you no to something, don't try to talk your pa into saying yes. That would make me very sad."

Without answering, MJ jumped off the sofa. "Come on, Pa, I want to show you a turtle I know!" He ran out the door.

Murphy chuckled. "You might have to repeat the dog thing." He gave her a long piercing look before he followed MJ.

It would be wonderful if words made a happy family. Her mind and her heart were warring against each other. It made everything confusing, and she didn't want to make a big mistake. Even though he hadn't abandoned her, they'd still been apart a long time. She would be nice to Murphy as she had promised. But she had questions. Did he still plan to add on to the house? There was already enough room for them. Would he still be here come harvest time?

She gave herself a mental shake. Her emotions had been high and she hadn't slept, and exhaustion was beginning to take its toll. Quickly, she walked to the kitchen and made two sandwiches, then set them on the table covered with a towel. After she was certain Murphy and MJ would have everything they needed for the noon meal, she climbed the stairs and practically fell into bed.

Everything was brighter now that MJ knew the truth. They went and saw the turtle, and then MJ decided he was hungry. As they walked back to the house, MJ kept glancing at him and smiling. "I'm glad you're here, Pa."

Murphy kneeled and took his son in his arms. "Me too, son." His eyes grew moist. He'd missed so much, but he had *now*. He stood, and MJ yawned. "I know, I'm tired too."

"How come it took so long to get to the Dooley place but not long to get home?"

"Guy took you to his house using a path that is much longer and it was dark, so everyone went slowly so the horses didn't step in a hole. Coming back, we used a path that was much, much shorter. Plus, we rode the horses."

MJ nodded. They went into the house and found that Brooke had prepared them sandwiches.

But had Brooke eaten? She was probably sleeping, but he wanted to be sure she hadn't gone missing. Leaving MJ eating, he went up the stairs and when he got to the entrance to her room he smiled. Lying on her side facing the door, she wore such a serene expression on her face. He hadn't realized it, but she was usually full of worry lately. It must be scary to think she had to run the farm herself and then to learn about all the lies. His wife was a powerful woman. He smiled as he quietly backed away and went down the steps.

"Is Ma sick?"

"She's just napping. I'm thinking it's a good idea."

"You do?" MJ frowned. "I guess I think so too."

Murphy would have to be careful. He'd never had such sway with anyone before. "I'll clean up here. Why don't you go on up and rest?"

"Women do the cleaning. I just leave the dishes."

"Well, MJ, I've learned in life that a person should help whenever they can. It'll only take a minute for me to clean up and maybe it'll make your ma smile when she sees that she doesn't have to wash dishes."

MJ nodded and went up the stairs.

Murphy cleaned up. What were his brothers doing? He missed them. He'd rather take Brooke and MJ back to the ranch, but he didn't want to lose Brooke. He'd ride to town tomorrow and mail a letter to his family. Yawning, he made his way to his room. It would be heaven to sleep beside his wife again. He'd have to keep reminding himself to take it slow. He lay down on his back and closed his eyes.

Thank you, Lord, for my many many blessings.

MURPHY WROTE his letter to his family and was on his way to mail it. Brooke didn't want to overhear any gossip, so she stayed at the farm with MJ. He just hoped she didn't try to do all the chores. The look in her eye was different this morning. The outright hostility was gone, but she remained wary. One day soon he hoped to see nothing but happiness in her eyes. That would probably take a bit of time.

His family would be happy for him, but he wasn't sure they'd understand his need to stay here. His nine brothers were on the Kavanagh ranch in Texas. He bet he wouldn't recognize some of their children since little ones grew so fast.

He hadn't gotten a good look at the town before, but now

he studied it. The place was just as small as his initial impression had given. He needed to talk to the lawyer and the banker alone, and he needed to do some shopping at the general store. Both Brooke and MJ could use new clothes. Maybe just a few items. It wouldn't do to overwhelm her and make her mad.

A familiar horse caught his eye. Was that bay Fitzpatrick's horse? Murphy rode to the horse and slid down off Nugget, then tied him to the hitching post and went around the big bay horse. Sure enough, it wore the Kavanagh brand. Where was Fitzpatrick? It was too early to be at the saloon.

He'd run into him, he figured, in a town as tiny as this. And he still had things to do. After Murphy took care of some business with the bank and the lawyer, he walked to the general store. He looked over the readymade dresses, confused by the sizes.

"Need some help?" asked a man's voice. "What color hair does your filly have?"

Laughing, Murphy turned and hugged Fitzpatrick. "What are you doing here?"

"I'm here to pry you away from whichever woman you're involved with and bring you home." Fitzpatrick laughed. "She'd best be mighty pretty."

Murphy frowned. "Most beautiful woman I know." He turned back to the dresses.

An older woman with a big smile hurried to him. "If you tell me her name, I might know her size."

"It's for my wife, Brooke Malery, well, actually her name is Brooke Kavanagh. I need a change of clothes for my son MJ. He's eight and average size I'd say."

"I'm Mrs. Harper. I haven't seen Brooke in a long while…"

"She's still the same size she was eight years ago."

A broad smile lit her face. "Why, you must be her dead soldier! It was so tragic, but now it's a miracle."

Fitzpatrick stood behind Mrs. Harper. His jaw dropped for a moment, then he shook his head.

Mrs. Harper took a dress off the rack. "This one should fit. The green will look lovely with her red hair. How many dresses do you need?"

"One for the time being. My wife is a very proud woman, and I think one is enough for now."

Fitzpatrick mouthed, "What?"

"Follow me for the boys' clothes." She walked across the store and picked up a pair of trousers and a blue button-down shirt. "What does the boy look like? Blue usually looks good on everyone."

Murphy grinned. "He looks just like me."

"Excuse me," Fitzpatrick interrupted, casting Murphy a sidelong glance. "I need to talk to my brother outside."

Murphy frowned. "We'll talk when I'm done. Mrs. Harper, this is my brother Fitzpatrick." Murphy walked to the ribbons next and selected a green one. He also picked up a wooden top for MJ. He put his things on the back counter and then added four peppermint sticks.

"Howdy, I'm Mr. Harper." The man's smile was bigger than his wife's.

"Murphy Kavanagh. Nice to meet you."

"Will this be all?" Mr. Harper asked.

"For now. We'll be back later in the week with the wagon to stock up." He handed the man cash. "I also have this letter of credit in case my wife or son need to purchase anything."

"I bet Mrs. Kavanagh is happy you're back from... Where was it you were?"

He let the question go unanswered and offered a smile instead. "It was nice to meet you." He gathered up his purchases and left the store. He was busy putting the packages in his saddlebags when his brother walked up.

"What is going on? A wife and a son? You'll ruin her reputation as soon as people find out you aren't married to her," Fitzpatrick hissed.

"I should have mailed the letter sooner." Murphy sighed. "I'm sorry I worried everyone. Want to meet my family?"

A frown creased Fitzpatrick's brow, but then he shrugged and nodded.

CHAPTER NINE

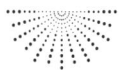

"Ma! Pa has someone with him!" MJ hollered.

"MJ, I'm right here. There's no need to shout." Brooke stepped around the clothesline that hid her. It had been wash day. She shook her head. Why did he have to bring someone home today? She was sweaty and dirty from scrubbing the clothes. There was no help for it now, though, as they rode into the yard. Murphy nodded to her.

She pulled her shoulders back and walked as properly as she could. "Hello Murphy. I see you brought a guest." She turned to his companion. "You must excuse my harried appearance. I was finishing up the wash. I'll just freshen up."

"Don't go," Murphy said. "It's just my brother, Fitzpatrick."

"Ma'am," he said as he tipped his hat.

"Is there something wrong at the ranch? Is someone sick?" she asked.

"No, ma'am. We just didn't know where Murphy had gotten himself off to."

Brooke glanced at Murphy. "Didn't he tell you where he was?"

"I finally got the information from the telegram that lawyer sent. Did you know telegrams are private? It took a bit of persuading. Murphy never mentioned a wife or son."

Her face heated in shame. She already knew he hadn't told his family, but she still felt humiliated. Her heart hurt. When would she ever learn? Fitzpatrick was probably here to take Murphy home and Murphy would go with him.

"If you'll excuse me, I'll make some coffee." She walked as fast as she could without it looking like she was fleeing. As soon as she entered the house, she heard MJ's excited voice. The contents of her stomach threatened to come back up. She put on the coffee to boil and ran up the steps to her room.

She had one other dress to wear, although it would be better used as a rag. Still, it would have to do. She washed her face and freshened up. Her hair refused to be tamed, but she needed to get downstairs, so she left it loose. When she got to the kitchen, Murphy was pouring the coffee.

"Would you like a cup?" he asked.

"Thank you." She sat at the table and smiled at MJ's enthusiasm. "Tell me, Fitzpatrick, are you married?"

He almost spit his coffee out. "Maybe if Murphy didn't steal all the single gals, I might have a chance. I swear all he does is sit on porches drinking lemonade with the prettiest gals."

She stiffened and took a sip of coffee to digest his words. Murphy had said he hadn't looked at any other women, even though he had thought her dead. And here was his brother painting a vastly different picture for her. Every time she turned around, there was another lie. It got to be tiresome trying to sort out the truth, and it was wearing her down.

"MJ, that means Murphy Junior, right?" Fitzpatrick stared at her as though she was some sort of criminal.

She quickly stood and muttered a few words about

getting supper started. If this was how his whole family behaved, she never wanted to meet them. Sounded as though Murphy had a happier life back in Texas with all the pretty gals.

She was cooking pot roast and wished she had more fresh vegetables to add to it. There was plenty of bread, though, and she ended up using the last of her jarred peaches in a cobbler. Did other adults wish they could just run away for a few days?

Murphy hadn't come in to deny what Fitzpatrick had said. It was disturbing. Murphy could have told her the truth of things. He had thought her dead, or so he said. Maybe his family expected him to marry a better, richer woman. She'd had it with men and how they changed things to suit them.

For six years she'd known Murphy was alive. For six years she wondered what she'd done to make him go away. Every night she tried to think of every conversation they'd had and where'd she'd gone wrong.

She'd taken the bullet out of him and nursed him back to health. They'd gotten on so well he had proposed to her. By that time, her heart was his. How many others had he "married" to have his husbandly rights? Despite what he told her, he must have dated, and from what Fitzpatrick said, Murphy was successful with women. That slashed her deeply. While she was taking care of their son and working the ranch as well as doing all the housework, he was charming ladies.

She put the pot roast to the side of the stove that wasn't too hot and walked out the back door. She needed to check on the wheat and make sure each seed was covered by dirt. That task would keep her busy for the rest of the day.

"Where did Ma go?" MJ asked, looking around.

"I'm sure she'll be right back in. She probably needed more water."

"But Pa, fetching water is my job."

"Your ma probably just wanted us men to have some time to ourselves."

MJ puffed out his chest. "Us men need our time."

Murphy and Fitzpatrick exchanged smiles.

"Gemma had another girl. They named her Pearl. Teagan sure does dote on his girls. Donnell and Clarissa's time is coming soon enough. The whole ranch is crawling with babies. Hey, do you think we could go to the saloon tonight?"

"Why? Do you have too much money in your pockets and need to lighten the load by giving it away playing cards?"

"Very funny."

"This farm will be mine someday," MJ said proudly. "I'm going to turn it into a cat ranch."

"Cats!" Fitzpatrick started laughing and couldn't seem to stop.

"I'll check on Ma." MJ walked out the front door, his shoulders slumped.

"Gee, Fitzpatrick, could you think before you speak?"

"What did I do?"

"You told my wife I was spending time with all the females and you laughed at MJ's cat ranch idea."

Fitzpatrick laughed again. "You have to admit it's funny."

"It's not funny to him."

"So, you're going along with this cat idea? Murphy, it's stupid and will never work. Why encourage something that will never happen?" Fitzpatrick poured himself more coffee. "Your woman makes excellent coffee."

"She is my wife," Murphy ground out.

"So you say."

"What's that supposed to mean?"

"Obviously, she had your son, but there's no way you

married her. Did she just decide to tell you about MJ because she needs your muscle to run the farm?"

The sun had started to set, and neither Brooke nor MJ had come back. Murphy loved his brother, but he had an enormous mouth and his foot landed in it often.

First Murphy went to the barn. MJ was probably with his cats. He spotted him in an empty stall. "It's starting to get dark. Are you coming in soon?"

"Is your brother still there? He's mean. And my cat ranch is not stupid!" MJ had tears in his eyes.

"Well you're right, Fitzpatrick can be mean, but I don't think he intends to be. Who cares what he thinks anyway? Let's have supper."

"Did Ma come back?" MJ's eye grew wide as he waited for an answer.

"I'm not sure where she is."

"She's under the willow tree. You might want to bring her blankets so she can sleep there. She can be mighty stubborn."

"Yes she can. Go on in and eat."

"Do I have to talk to your brother?" He sounded glum.

"Just ignore him for now. I'll be back as soon as I can."

MJ raced off to the house. Fitzpatrick hadn't been here but a few hours and already he had everyone upset. Murphy started walking toward the budding tree and sure enough, there was his wife. What was he supposed to say?

"I'm sorry my brother upset you."

She didn't look up. "It wasn't only him, he just has a big mouth. It's you who has me crying my eyes out. You know something, Murphy? I'm done. I'm done crying and wondering what I did wrong or why you didn't come and get me. I just got over that, and accepted that you were tricked by my father. But your brother probably knows you better than anyone and it sure sounds like you are a ladies man." She lifted her head and pinned him in her stare. "I bet if not for MJ, you'd have ridden out by now. Are you planning to sell the farm after all?"

"I already told you I don't want to sell," he muttered.

"Because if you sell it, I need to make plans for MJ and me. It's a good thing Fitzpatrick came here. I was looking at you with stars in my eyes. I don't have time for dreams, I only have time to be realistic." She gave him a sad smile. Her eyes were red rimmed from what must have been quite a bout of crying.

He released a sigh, silently cursing his brother. "Fitzpatrick tends to exaggerate."

"So you never sat on a woman's porch and drank lemonade?"

"It was water."

She stared at him. "You know I finally thought maybe you didn't tell your family about getting married because of your grief and that just maybe my pa lied to you. You almost had me believing you. I'm the biggest fool in Arkansas. And I can't afford to be foolish. I have my son to raise. Just give me a little warning before I have to be off the farm." She stood and shook out her skirt to get the dirt off. She looked as though she had more to say, but she just turned and walked back to the house.

How gullible could a person be? She had believed her pa all those years ago, but then she had been coming to believe Murphy. Was she so needy that she believed lies if they made her feel good? She had to make better choices, especially for MJ. It sounded as though Murphy had plenty of women and that made her insides twist. He didn't know what lonely was.

Thank goodness God was giving her the strength to avoid temptation. Not that she was alone because she wasn't. It was her heart and soul crying out for what she'd once had with Murphy. But that was in the past, and this was a case of once something was gone it couldn't be gotten back.

He'd said again that he didn't want to sell her farm. If he was telling the truth, she would put her foot down and demand he build a house of his own. It hurt too much having him so close to her. She had better things to use her energy on. Then again, maybe Fitzpatrick would convince him to go home. But MJ would lose his father again. It didn't matter what she thought, her heart hurt something awful. There had been times over the years when gazing at MJ made her heart ache for what she'd lost.

A lamp was lit in the house, and she could see Fitzpatrick and MJ talking and laughing. She didn't want to see Fitzpatrick, but she didn't have a choice. She dove deep inside of herself and gathered her courage. She smiled at the two as she entered the house.

"Looks like you have been having fun. I hate to say this, but MJ it's bedtime."

"See ya tomorrow, Uncle Fitzpatrick." MJ ran up the stairs. She lit another lamp and followed him up.

Not thinking, she opened the door and walked into MJ's room.

"Ma, I'm getting changed." He looked appalled, as though she had never helped him before.

She quickly turned her back. "I'm sorry. I should have knocked, but I thought it would be too dark for you to see. Would you like a story and then I could hear your prayers?"

"Ma, I'm too old to be hanging on your skirts. I'll see you in the morning." He opened the door and after she went through, he closed it behind her.

Stunned, she just stood in the hall. What had just happened? Where was her little boy? Just last night he'd wanted a story and she always listened to his prayers. She walked into her room and put the lamp on the table next to her bed. Was this MJ's way of telling her he was leaving with Murphy? No! She wouldn't allow it. Maybe she needed to tell Murphy to leave. Fear *filled* her. She couldn't do that either, for he'd win if he tried to take MJ.

The reality of the situation was she was the outsider. This wasn't her farm anymore. Oh, Pa, what a mess you left me in. She heard Murphy come into the house and talk to Fitzpatrick, but their voices were too soft for her to hear.

She pulled her dress over her head and hung it on a peg. Next, she washed and put on her nightgown. She turned down the covers and glanced outside. Guy Dooley was up in a tree watching her. Swiftly she left the room, ran down the stairs, grabbed the rifle and raced outside. Taking aim, she shot at Guy and missed, though she hit the tree.

Murphy was behind her, trying to wrestle the rifle from her.

"What are you doing?" he shouted angrily.

"Protecting myself." She pushed Fitzpatrick back with her shoulder and went back inside. She trembled as she walked up the steps.

"Brooke, come back down here. You need to explain why you were running around in your nightgown with the gun."

Ignoring him, she went to her room and locked the door. Instead of asking who was out there, he was concerned about her nightgown? He probably thought her crazy. She pressed her back along the wall, inching slowly to the window. Her legs felt wobbly as she snuck a peek. She didn't see Guy.

Sighing in relief, she relaxed her tense shoulders. How many times in the past had Guy watched her? He'd probably seen more of her than she had. A chill coursed through her. It didn't matter whether she had a man around. Guy didn't seem to care. Riding out to talk to his mother again might be the best idea. Then if he still spied on her again, she'd see the sheriff.

Her bed called out to her, but she pulled a wooden chair over to the window and kept watch. Someone needed to protect her and MJ.

CHAPTER TEN

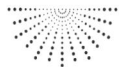

Murphy, Fitzpatrick, and MJ ate a breakfast of eggs and bacon they'd cooked. MJ took his plate to the counter.

"Think I should see about Ma?"

Murphy shook his head. "Let's let her sleep." He stared at Fitzpatrick.

"MJ, how about you show me the beginnings of your cat ranch?" Fitzpatrick asked.

"Oh, boy! Once you see it, you'll understand it."

Murphy heard MJ talking about little cats as they walked out of the house. Murphy went up the stairs and lightly knocked on Brooke's door. When there wasn't an answer, he opened the door and walked in. She sat in a chair by the window with her head slumped forward, though she seemed to have a good grip on the rifle.

He took the rifle from her first and that woke her. The glare she gave him was unexpected, and he jerked backward. What had he done? She was the one running around in her nightgown in front of his brother. There must be something wrong with her. How had he missed that?

She tilted her head and squinted at him. "What do you want?" She sounded weary.

"For starters, what was last night about?"

She huffed and then she stood. "It was about protecting myself and MJ. I'm sick to think I've been spied on. He probably watched as I changed my clothes." Her lip quivered.

"Who? I don't understand." Should he just go along with what she says? It might be easier.

"I'd just put on my nightgown when I thought I saw a face in the tree, the one I shot. It was Guy and he was looking in my window."

Anger at the other man rushed through Murphy. Was that it, or should he wait for more?

"I scared him off when I shot at him, but I figured he'd come back so I waited all night by the window with my rifle. You and Fitzpatrick thought the entire thing funny. If he'd been watching you in your most private moments you'd be upset too." She sat on the edge of the bed. "This isn't working for me, having you here. MJ has changed too much, and I... I'm miserable. I'm going into town today to find some work and a place to live." She punched the bed. "Why does the law have to be so complicated? I've worked this farm all my life. It's in my blood. Yet our marriage gives the whole place to you." She quickly glanced away.

"As your husband, yes, it legally belongs to me. I have no idea what your father thought or why he lied to me about your supposed death. But now that I'm here, it's plain as can be that you need help to run the farm."

"I never looked at another man, not even when I decided I should find another husband. And after I found out you were alive, my father reminded me constantly that I was married and couldn't find another husband. He made me feel shame for something I never did. Men can do what they want. They can sit on another women's porch and no one says a word. I got the feeling that you've become quite the ladies' man." She huffed out a frustrated breath. "Don't feel that you need to stay here each night. If our vows aren't sacred to you, then just forget it."

Murphy stared at her, one eyebrow raised. "Does this mean you plan to find a beau?" he asked quietly.

She glared again. "It's not something I feel I can do. I'd want to be honest to any man I became friends with and that would mean telling him about you. I'm sure your brother was sent here to bring you home. Well, I don't want to leave here, but if you sell, at least give me a bit of notice before I need to pack up." She stood and went to the door. She held on to the knob. "I'm going to get dressed. I have a visit I must make today."

Murphy stepped out of her room. The door closed hard behind him. He went to the kitchen and poured himself more coffee. *She's making this all my fault. I didn't have any hand in making this mess. I thought she believed that I thought her dead. Could she be having a breakdown?*

Oh Lord, I just found her. Please don't make it so I have to send her away.

Brooke walked down the stairs in her old patched dress.

"I can cook you some breakfast," he offered.

"No, I need to take care of something."

MJ ran into the house and instead of hugging her, he just said the quickest good morning he'd ever heard. Murphy frowned.

"Murphy, may I talk to you alone?" Brooke asked. "Perhaps in the barn... that is, if Fitzpatrick will stay with MJ."

"I ain't no baby!" MJ insisted, staring her down.

Brooke turned and ran out of the house.

"MJ, we will have a brief talk about manners and mothers when I get back." Murphy ignored MJ's scowl. He'd deal with it later. Right now, he needed to see if his wife was actually crazy or not.

"I'm not sure where to start," Brooke said as she paced. "My priority is MJ. Did you know he wouldn't allow me to tuck him in, read to him, or hear his prayers last night?" Her voice wavered, but she didn't care. "He barely said anything to me this morning. What did you say to him? Are you planning on taking him from me?"

Murphy took a step toward her, reached out and with his hand lifted her chin so their gazes met. "I would never take him from you." His stare was intense, and he didn't stop until she nodded. "I'll talk to him about it."

"Ever since you came here, you have turned everything around. I owned a farm, kept a roof over my head with the ability to feed me and my son. Now I'm going to town to find a job. I know you don't believe me about Guy last night, but he was out there. I'm stopping at his mother's house on my way back. You can tell Fitzpatrick he can take you home soon. Best you just leave. Maybe you could find someone to lease this land from you."

"No."

"Then you *are* selling it?" She cocked her left brow.

A scowl twisted his face and he scratched his temple as though deep in thought. "Listen, I don't know where you're getting all these crazy ideas from."

"Crazy? Who — You know what? Fine, think or do what you want. I need to get started on my day." She went to Maisey's stall and led her out of it. Then she saddled the horse herself. When she looked over her shoulder, Murphy was gone. Why wouldn't he just give her a straight answer about the farm?

She rode toward town. What did he mean about her crazy ideas? She needed to get a job today. Didn't he realize she would need to work once she no longer had the farm?

She tied the horse to a hitching post and stopped in at every shop and restaurant. No one needed help. Her spirit was flailing as she trudged back to Maisey.

"Mrs. Kavanagh! Mrs. Kavanagh," An older gentleman called. She stopped and waited.

"It's nice to see you again, Mr. Attwood." She gave him a smile.

"I hope I'm not presuming too much, but I heard mention from Tom Faber's receptionist that you need a job, and my housekeeper needed to be with her family. The job is cleaning and cooking. There is a separate house for you and your son to live in."

"Would cooking include feeding all your cowhands?" His ranch was vast.

"No, we have a chow hall next to the bunk house. You would only cook for me, yourself and your son. I know... Actually, I don't know what you are going through. If you need a job, you have one."

Lenny Attwood was one of the nicest men she'd ever met. "I'll take the job. How soon do you need me?"

"How about I send out a few men with a wagon tomorrow afternoon? Do you think you could be packed up by then?"

"Yes, Mr. Attwood. Thank you so very much." Her eyes welled.

He awkwardly patted her shoulder. "I'm sure it'll be fine."

"Yes, I'll see you tomorrow."

He tipped his hat at her and she watched as he walked away. That sure was lucky. She took Maisey's reins and mounted the horse. As soon as she was out of town, she took her bonnet off. She wanted to feel the wind in her hair. It was a beautiful day.

Thank you, Lord, I know I said it was lucky, but I know it was You opening a door for me and MJ. I really don't know what the future will bring, but knowing You walk beside me gives me the greatest comfort.

Stopping at the Dooleys would be a waste of time since she was moving tomorrow. The thrill of having a job faded as the hurt of leaving Murphy took over. She'd been without him for years before, though, so she could do it again. He could finally go home to his ranch.

As she rode up to the old farmhouse, it saddened her to know she had to leave. It would have been different if she couldn't make a go of the farm. Instead, it seemed best to just admit to herself that the place didn't belong to her anymore. She bet the house at the Attwood ranch would be lovely. She had always liked Mr. Attwood; he had great manners and there was kindness in his eyes.

She'd have to leave her animals, but she planned to take Maisey unless Murphy pushed the fact that she didn't belong to her anymore. There really wasn't any reason she shouldn't be packed tonight. Apprehension went through her. Telling MJ would be the worst part.

An unfamiliar buggy was parked in front of the house. Fitzpatrick came out of the barn and helped her off Maisey's back. "I'll take care of your horse."

She stared at the buggy as she cautiously made her way to the door. Something was going on, and she had a feeling it wasn't good.

She ran her hands down her patched dress and walked into the house. She stopped and put her bonnet on the table near the door while she took a deep breath.

"Well, hello," she greeted as she offered a polite smile.

Murphy and the other man stood. "Brooke, this is Dr. Hunt. He's here to see about your health."

She furrowed her brow. What was going on? "Dr. Hunt, it's nice to meet you. Would you like some coffee?"

"I already have it boiling, and MJ is in the barn with Fitzpatrick. We've been waiting for you to get back."

She sat down. "What about my health?"

The doctor cleared his voice. "I'm here to see if you're sane or insane."

She stood back up and crossed her arms in front of her. She glared at Murphy. "Did you ask the doctor to come here to see if I'm mad? How dare you?" She turned to the doctor. "I'm afraid your time has been wasted. I'm fine. In fact, I'm moving out tomorrow so I'll no longer have to listen to Mr. Kavanagh."

"I see. Where is it you think you're going tomorrow?" The tone of his voice had her doubting herself.

"I found a job. Mr. Attwood has hired me to be his housekeeper. He even has an empty house MJ and I can live in." She lifted her chin.

"What if I told you there wasn't a Mr. Attwood?" He cocked his left brow as he stared at her.

"I'd have to say you're the one who is mad. I just spoke to him in town."

"Did you stop to see this Guy fellow who watches you?" He leaned forward, waiting.

"I did not. I'm not going to be here, so I thought it a waste of time. I wanted to get back, to pack." She bit her lip as she watched the two men exchange glances.

"I can see how agitated you are. Won't you sit back down?" the doctor asked.

"Murphy, what is going on? Is this so you can steal MJ from me? Is it because I didn't fall into your arms when you showed up? Is it because I really don't want to leave Arkansas and live on your family ranch? Or perhaps you have another woman in Texas. Tell you what, you live your life and I'll live mine. I will be off your farm tomorrow afternoon. Both MJ and I will live at the Attwood Ranch. Now, I don't know what's going on, but I've known Mr. Attwood for half my life." Her face must be tomato red, judging by how warm it was.

"Now, dear, don't get hysterical. There is also the matter of the physical examination." Dr. Hunt had a gleam in his eyes. "We can do that at my… hospital."

She backed up slowly. "Murphy, please send MJ to me once this sorry excuse for a doctor is gone." She turned and raced up the stairs and into her room. It took a minute to find the key and then she locked it.

Her heart was pounding hard against her chest. What had just happened? They seem to make a case for a judge to have her committed. She noticed a pretty green dress on her bed and sat so she could touch it. Was this her going to the mad house dress? Murphy was the crazy one if he thought these tactics would work. She just needed to get to Mr. Attwood's, to prove she really had been hired.

How did one prove they weren't insane? She'd have to have witnesses to say she was fine. Now she wished she'd made an effort to make friends. She had Robin, but half the town didn't trust her and her cures. Brooke had rarely gone to town until her father had died. MJ knew she was fine, of course, but who would take the word of an immature boy? Fitzpatrick was probably the one who had the doctor come to the house. If she had put a wrap on before she shot at Guy, would it have made a difference?

Her shoulders slumped and she thought she might be sick. They couldn't take her away, could they? She never would have thought Murphy would be involved in something so sinister. Hysterical? Murphy had seldom gone to town during his stay. He'd never met or heard of Mr. Attwood, she bet. No wonder he thought there isn't such a man. She'd heard horrible things go on at the madhouse. Would they lock her in a dark room for months?

Suddenly, her room seemed too small; she was trapped. She'd locked herself in with no way to escape. She wanted to weep, but she didn't have time. If she ran for it, she'd have to leave MJ behind. Her father had always told her to live, to fight another day. If she allowed them to take her away, she'd never see MJ again.

How far was it to the ground if she left through her window? She walked to it and looked. She could do it. Suddenly she spotted Guy in the tree again. Disgust filled her as she sat on her bed to think.

CHAPTER ELEVEN

Murphy was tired of listening to the doctor. Once again, Fitzpatrick had talked him into doing something that was turning out disastrous. He excused himself and climbed the stairs. Once outside Brooke's room he knocked and tried to turn the knob. He frowned.

"Brooke, I'm sorry. There is nothing wrong with you. Please unlock the door." He put his ear to the door to listen. He heard sniffling.

"Is Dr. Hunt gone?" she asked.

"No, the thing is, we offered him lodging for the night." He heard a gasp and maybe a growl?

"Fine, I'll talk to you once he's gone. I'm going to take a nap now. My brain has been so taxed. I'm sure you understand." Her voice was laced in sarcasm.

It would take days to get her to forgive him, maybe weeks. There wasn't anything he could do about it at the moment. Where had Fitzpatrick found this doctor? How many women had he sent to hospitals? He pretty much told Brooke everything she said was made up. Hopefully Murphy could persuade Brooke to eat something later.

He should have objected to the questions. He should have just said she *was* sane and put an end to the nonsense. So she had really found a job. It was like getting kicked in the stomach. Murphy needed her present to work things out. He wanted his family. He'd already bought the property next to the farm to run cattle on. His next plan was to have a sizeable house built on the border of both properties, and he wanted both Brooke and MJ to stay with him for always.

How did everything go from hopeful to hopeless so fast? He'd been within sight of his dream, and now his dream had disappeared. He ran his hand over his face. She had only just begun to trust him, and now she had no reason to trust him one bit. He would have to let her go tomorrow. But he wasn't going back to Texas, not when he had a big spread right next door. He'd get that up and going. How long would it take for her to forgive him?

"You really blew it, Murphy," Fitzpatrick said. He shook his head as he sat down in a chair on the porch.

"Where did you find that doctor?"

"I asked around in town and sent for him. He's not cheap, you know."

Murphy narrowed his eyes. "What do you mean you asked around? There isn't a doctor in town?"

"Sure there's a doctor, but he refused to get involved. Too many men say their wives are crazy to get rid of them." He shrugged. "So I asked in the saloon and most of the folks there thought Dr. Hunt was the doctor we needed." A smile spread across his face.

"Do you realize what you've done? I wanted an actual doctor. I don't want to have her proclaimed mad. Now Dr. Hunt plans to take her away tomorrow. I'm not trying to be rid of her. I want her to want me to stay. I have a family and I want us to live as a family. Brooke got an excellent job at the Attwood spread."

"That's the biggest ranch around, according to folks at the saloon," offered Fitzpatrick. "The owner lost his wife not too long ago. He probably thinks your wife is single."

Murphy's frustration built. "Fitzpatrick, were you kicked in the head by a mule?"

"Why would you even ask such a thing? I've done everything I know how to make you happy."

"Happy?" Murphy sputtered.

"Yes, I want you home. You were happy there. My plan was to get Brooke out of the picture. You two don't even like each other. Then you could sell the farm and take MJ home. I could see your struggle with Brooke. She is beautiful and she's a feisty one. I wonder if it's because she has red hair. She's too smart for her own good and she's capable of profiting from working this farm. You were in a jam, and I helped you." Fitzpatrick sounded rather proud of himself.

Murphy concentrated on his breathing. He was so angry he was afraid he'd hurt his brother. They had always wrestled at home, but they pulled their punches. He wanted to punch Fitzpatrick, a lot. He slowed his breathing and tried to hold his anger in. When had he ever said Brooke was in the way? Oh no, was it because he said a wife would be a millstone around his neck? He said many things to get out of courting anyone. He'd often told Fitzpatrick he did not want a wife ever. Now his words were haunting him.

BROOKE HUGGED a pillow to herself and rocked back and forth. Repeating over and over, *"Be strong and courageous. Do not be afraid or terrified because of them, for the LORD your God goes with you; He will never leave you nor forsake you."*

She put the pillow back and closed the curtains. Guy was

still there, but she wouldn't ask for his help. She wouldn't try to jump out the window. She would put her faith in God.

After changing into her nightgown, she went into MJ's room. His hair was tousled, and he appeared to be so peaceful. What had he thought of the last few days? Did he know Murphy planned to send her away tomorrow? It was common knowledge when a person went into an asylum they never came back. For some reason, God seemed to want her to be taken away. Surely, though, He would protect her child.

She left the room and slowly closed the door so as not to make noise. She went back to her room and as she opened the door she was pulled inside. At first, she thought it was , but it was the doctor instead. She pushed at him, but he was much stronger than he appeared. He put his hand over her mouth and held her.

"You don't have to go tomorrow, you know. I could change my mind." He changed his hold on her and touched her face with one hand, inhaling deeply. "With the proper… persuasion."

She squirmed and then bit his hand. With a snarl, he let go and she bolted from the room. She practically flew down the stairs and into Murphy's brawny arms.

"Hey, what's wrong?" he asked, softly.

"He—he—he grabbed me in my room." She couldn't help the tears that fell.

"Who? Guy?"

"No, the doctor." She shivered.

Fitzpatrick was by her side in an instant.

"What? Are you sure?" Fitzpatrick asked.

Murphy held her close. "Tell me."

"I went to look in on MJ and the doctor was in my room when I returned." Her legs felt wobbly. "I need to sit down."

She gave a brief cry when the doctor came down the

stairs. She grabbed a quilt and wrapped it around her, then huddled in the corner of the sofa.

Dr. Hunt tilted his head and then righted it as he stared at her. "This happens. I'm not surprised. I should have insisted on sleeping down here. Brooke, surely—"

"It's Mrs. Kavanagh, and I refuse to allow you to twist everything I do or say into something not normal. You know you were in my room and you told me you might change your mind about me having to leave, that you could be *persuaded*. I didn't give you a chance to tell me how I could change your mind. I have my suspicions."

"I'll go get my bag. I can give her a sedative. This often happens." Dr. Hunt turned to go upstairs.

"Don't take another step," Murphy growled.

Fitzpatrick started for the stairs. "I'll get your things, Hunt. Your services are no longer required."

"I can't leave!" he blustered. "It's dark."

Fitzpatrick acted as though he didn't hear the doctor and hurried upstairs.

Murphy grabbed Brooke's rifle from above the mantel and kept it trained on Dr. Hunt. "I can't understand how I could have believed you!"

"You believed me because I'm right and because you wanted her gone. It's easier to send a wife away than it is to kill her."

She gasped and swallowed hard. She didn't want to believe him, but…

MJ ran down the stairs and hopped onto the couch and then put his arms around her. "My ma is staying here with me. The rest of you can go. We were just fine before any of you came!" He turned toward her and whispered, "Right Ma?"

Brooke nodded at her brave boy. When she glanced at Murphy, he looked as though he'd been slapped in the face.

As soon as they got rid of the doctor, she'd have MJ tell Murphy he didn't mean him.

Fitzpatrick's steps were louder than usual as he came down. He threw the doctor's belongings out beyond the porch and then took the doctor by the scruff of his neck and threw him out too. He slammed the door and then locked it.

"Brooke I'm sorry for my part in all this. I'm going upstairs to Murphy's room." He didn't wait for an answer.

Murphy put the rifle back and then he sat on the couch. He tried to put his arm around his son, but MJ shrugged it off.

Murphy's stomach lurched as though he'd been punched in his gut. He changed seats, so he sat opposite his family. "I'm not sure what to say. MJ, I love you and no amount of rejection from you will ever change that. Grownups make mistakes, and I made a big one. I'm sorry you had to take sides between your ma and me. I admire the way you stuck up for your ma. It's a sign you're becoming a fine man." He'd hoped for a bit of softening from them both, but they still glared at him.

"Brooke, I've been thrown off kilter ever since I saw you at the lawyer's office. I really believed you were dead. I didn't look at another woman once since I got to Texas after the war. You always filled my heart. It was especially hard loving you so much and feeling cheated we didn't have enough time together. I relived every day we had together over and over. I couldn't bear to hear your name. That is why I didn't tell my family. I needed to grieve in private. Did I sit on a porch or two? Yes, I did, but mainly to make Fitzpatrick mad. He thinks women should fall at his feet. So far none have."

He shifted in his seat. Their glares were lessening. "I

came to Arkansas alone so I could have my memories to myself. The first thing I did was visit a grave I was told was yours. It was a hard journey to make. When I found you alive, I wanted what we had before I had to go back to war, but you believe what your father told you. Thinking about it, why wouldn't you believe him? As far as you were concerned, he'd never lied. It devastated me that you didn't want me in your life. And when I saw MJ—well, I never knew my heart could expand so big to hold the love I have for both of you."

"You wanted to send my ma away!" MJ clenched his fists.

"I never wanted her to leave. I was concerned that something might be wrong. Fitzpatrick agreed with me and pointed out things I never noticed. I never intended to have your ma declared insane and sent away."

Brooke's eyes went wide, and she licked her lips. Her chest still rose and fell rapidly, but Murphy thought he might be making progress.

"I am not sending your ma away," Murphy repeated. "If she has any problems, we will work through them together, but I am beginning to think I've made some mistakes. I don't want to send her away, and I also don't want to leave you or your ma again."

MJ glanced up at his mother. She put her arms around him and pulled him close. "Your father and I are married, and they are sacred vows we said before God. We need to try as hard as we can to get along. I even found a job with a house we could use, but we'll stay here instead. I want to make a go of this farm. It'll be yours someday, MJ." She glanced at Murphy as if she wanted to add something but then glanced away. "I think it's time for bed. I'll tuck you in, MJ."

Murphy stood. "I'll see you both in the morning." He was pleasantly surprised when MJ ran to him and gave him a quick hug around his legs before he ran up the stairs. He turned away when he realized a tear was trailing down his face.

He needed fresh air. He walked out onto the porch and studied the trees in front of Brooke's window. He stared, closed his eyes, and looked again. There was Guy sitting high in one of the trees. Murphy glanced at the window and was relieved Brooke had pulled the curtains closed. He tiptoed toward the tree.

"Ahem! Nice night for tree climbing?"

Guy startled and almost fell, but he was able to grab onto a branch and steady himself. "A little birdy told me you didn't think I'd be back. I've been waiting to see if Brooke needed help climbing out of the window."

Murphy frowned. "It's time for you to go home, Guy." He realized yelling wouldn't help.

"Yes sir, Mr. Kavanagh!" He climbed down and ran toward his home.

Murphy shook his head and felt worse than he already had. He needed to talk to Brooke tomorrow. They needed to figure out what in tarnation was going on.

CHAPTER TWELVE

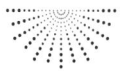

The atmosphere in the house was tense, but Brooke kept a smile on her face for MJ's sake. Fitzpatrick had been sent to the Attwood place to explain why she wouldn't be accepting the job. She was almost done cooking breakfast when Murphy and MJ came out of the barn. MJ was chattering, and Murphy had a big grin on his face.

Her heart smiled as she watched the two of them.

"Ma! Guess what?" MJ yelled as he ran into the house.

"What?"

"Pa said another big cat I didn't even know is in the hayloft ready to have her little cats!"

"How exciting. Maybe you could give some kittens away." She placed the platter with scrambled eggs and bacon on the table.

Both MJ and Murphy stared at her with their mouths gaping.

"Ma! I need the little cats for my cat ranch."

"Oh. I'll let your Pa handle it. He's a rancher." She chuckled. "I have confidence you'll have your cat ranch up and going in no time."

Murphy looked surprised and startled at the same time. He probably hadn't given it a thought about who would tell MJ they couldn't keep all the kittens.

"Let's eat while it's still hot." They held hands and said grace. She silently praised God for being at her side.

"Thank you for the lovely green dress. It's, well, you know how it's been. Only necessities are purchased. I'm thankful and for the matching ribbon." She blushed when Murphy grinned at her.

"I got new clothes to wear too, Ma! Two new shirts and two pants. Pa said he'd get me new shoes too. He didn't know my size. And he got me a wooden top to play with." She was happy that MJ was so excited, but there was still a part of her that had doubts.

"I have credit at the general store you're to use."

"Oh, I couldn't—"

"You're my wife, and it would please me if you bought whatever you need."

She nodded, but she didn't intend to use his credit.

"I was wondering if just the two of us could go on a picnic?"

"Aw," MJ folded his arms in front of him.

"I'll take you fishing tomorrow, MJ," Murphy told him.

MJ smiled.

Brooke frowned. "MJ, I don't like your attitude. You got mad because you weren't included. I call the way you acted disrespectful. Tell your pa you're sorry."

MJ instantly looked contrite. "I'm sorry, Pa."

"I'm glad you apologized. It wouldn't have been fun fishing alone." Murphy nodded at MJ and then smiled at her. "Will you have time to make a picnic? I could help."

"I can do it. You two can check on the wheat. If you know what to check for."

"I knew I was coming back here after the war and I asked every farmer I met about farming. Come along MJ, we have a crop to tend." He smiled at them both.

She watched them leave, MJ running circles around Murphy as they walked. This is what she had imagined her life would be. It could be wonderful, but just yesterday the plan had been to get rid of her. They needed this picnic. There was much to discuss.

MURPHY SMILED as he helped Brooke onto her horse. She was wearing pants under her new dress. She even wore the ribbon in her hair and somehow, she appeared younger.

With Fitzpatrick staying at the house watching MJ, they could take their time. He smiled at her as they rode toward the river.

Please God, let both of our hearts be open. We said holy vows and I need guidance to win her love. I need to convince her I love her. I want her to finally believe I'm not a liar. Any help You can give me would be much appreciated.

Brooke glanced at him when they reached the river. "Where to?"

"Let's get down and lead the horses near those trees over there. Privacy would be nice for a change." Her face became a delightful rosy color. It turned brighter red when he lifted her down. She certainly wasn't immune to him.

He took her hand and entwined their fingers as they walked along the river. When they reached the trees, he stopped. He took everything they needed off the horses before he found them a nice grassy area.

"You're as pretty as sunshine on a summer's day."

She laughed. "Those are sweet words, Murphy."

He grinned at her. He laid out the blanket and put the basket in the middle. They both sat watching the water flow in the river. Now that he had Brooke alone, he wasn't sure how to start.

"I hope you're hungry." She set out bread, cheese, pickles along with raspberry jam.

"Looks good. I'm so sorry about yesterday. I was concerned about you and I should have trusted my gut. You would never have left the farm. I already figured out that since Fitzpatrick thought it a good idea, it wasn't. I'm supposed to protect you and it kills me the doctor was in your room. It's probably worked for him in the past. I bet he double crossed the women and took them to the asylum anyway. I should have gone to see your friend Robin about the questions I had. Can you forgive me?"

"Of course, I can and do. I've been at fault too. I didn't believe you when you came here. I'd been hurting for years because I thought you abandoned me. It took a bit for me to believe that my father had lied. I can be hardheaded. Sometimes it near killed me thinking you were making another family for yourself. And my hurt went deeper as I watched MJ growing up without a father. I'd given up on men. I grieved for you a long time and then when my father told me you were alive but hadn't come for me, rage took over my grief. I was angry with myself for believing in you when we married." She put food on her plate, but she didn't eat.

"I bought the land next to your farm. I thought we could expand by farming and ranching. Also, the farm belongs to you. I signed it over to you."

Her breath caught and she stared at him.

He took her hand and stroked the back of it with his thumb.

Her eyes widened. "Why didn't you tell me?"

"I was afraid you'd ask me to leave."

She gave him a quick nod. "You wanted to know your son. I can understand."

"No, not only MJ. I wanted to be near you too. I kept thinking I'd wake up and find it was all a dream. No one tells a husband and father that his wife died unless it's the truth. I think he was afraid I was there to take you back to Texas with me. I had made no decisions at that point. I wanted us to decide together. The farm, the ranch, it didn't matter as long as I had you. Your father stole that time from me. I could have loved you and watched our son grow." His voice began to get hoarse.

"I'm glad you never remarried. You being here has mended my broken heart. I meant what I said about trying to work it out. I take our vows seriously." She glanced away. "Do you…? I mean, had you planned to go back to Texas this time? I know you bought land but your family is there."

He put his plate aside and lifted her onto his lap. "My family is right here. I know how you feel about the farm and now we have plenty of land."

"Enough for a cat ranch?" She glanced at him, her eyes full of mirth.

He chuckled. "Do you think he'll outgrow this idea of his?"

"He's had this idea for a while. It will take something very exciting to change his mind."

He chuckled. "Maybe he wants to be a cowboy."

"Like his father." She tucked her head under his chin and gloried in the feeling of his warm, strong arms around her. It was a feeling of being safe, not being alone and a feeling of love. She closed her eyes. Would it last? They'd never really lived as man and wife. What if he decided he didn't like her? It was easy to dream about wonderful things, but reality was different. He'd called her beautiful, said he wanted to be near her. But he had never said he loved her. Still, she would try to be a good wife.

What would I have done without faith? You were the only one I could tell my troubles to. Just knowing You are always protecting me and loving me gave me serenity in my darkest days. I thank You, Lord, for all the miracles I have witnessed lately. You have taught me to see miracles in the little things. I'm not even mad at my father anymore. You brought my husband home and You gave me a fine son. I couldn't ask for anything more.

His arms tightened around her. "What are you thinking about?"

"All the ways God has blessed us. His guidance brought us to this very place."

"Your faith was always unwavering. I admire that. You can teach both me and MJ about faith."

"I'm no expert but I'd be happy to tell you about God's teachings."

"I love you." He pulled back and searched her eyes. He appeared certain.

"I love you too. I wasn't sure you would say the words. I can feel my entire body tingling. Love is a mighty thing. We have things to work out. Which side of the bed you'll sleep on. Who does what chores." She laughed. "I finally found myself a worker!"

"MJ is very good at giving orders." He smiled and then kissed her soft lips.

"Are you sure you want to settle here? I know you love the Texas ranch."

"We could always visit. I know how much you love this farm. Let's make it work."

"With the three of us and God's help, it will work." She smiled up at him and then stood. "We need to get back to our son."

"I like that—our son."

"Yes, our son and the cat ranch."

EPILOGUE

It had been a long scorching summer. Brooke sat on the front porch drinking a glass of water. The wheat was growing just fine. Her garden was yielding more than usual. The world was a glorious place thanks to God. Their new house was just about done. She wasn't allowed to see it. MJ watched her like a hawk. She took a long drink and went to the willow tree.

"Pa, I don't know what you were thinking. I forgive you for lying. It does me no good to have hate in my heart for you. Maybe hate is too strong of a word. Everything worked out the way it was supposed to work. I love both you and Ma." She turned and watched her family walk toward her.

"But Pa, I need all the cats. You said I could have a cat ranch."

Brooke tried not to laugh. Murphy could wiggle his way out of that one without her help. She laughed and it felt good. There had been a lot of love and laughter in her life lately. She didn't feel older than her time anymore. She was a young, newly wedded woman as far as she was concerned.

Both Murphy and MJ joined her on the porch. Murphy

kissed her cheek before he sat down.

"Pa, you can't wrangle up the cats. They need to roam free."

"I just thought we could build something like a chicken coop but bigger. This way you can keep track of the cats. You can let them out during the day."

"Will they come back each night?"

Murphy glanced at her. "I really don't know but if we leave out bowls of milk at night, I bet they'll come."

MJ frowned as he mulled the idea over. "It's a fine idea, Pa. I might even make you a partner!"

"Are we ready to show your ma her surprise?"

MJ's eyes grew wide as he nodded his head. "Finally, it was the hardest thing I've ever done. Keeping a secret is hard."

Murphy stood and reached out for her hand. She always marveled at how much bigger his hands were than hers. She couldn't have asked for a more attentive husband. He took all of her loneliness away.

They walked toward the new house. MJ ran ahead.

She was speechless. It was beautiful. The porch was huge and a table sat on one side with chairs around it. It would be lovely to eat outside. It always got too hot, and often her appetite fled. The front door was thick and it had an intricately carved K into it. She traced her fingers over it in awe.

She shrieked as Murphy swung her up into his sturdy arms. MJ opened the door.

"You're right, she likes this threshold thing."

Murphy gave him a smile when he set her down. "Go ahead, look around."

It was big and it had all new furniture in it. The carved banister caught her eye. "Did you do this?"

"Yes, ma'am."

She gasped when she came to the scrolled mantel above

the massive fireplace. The kitchen had a pantry and built-in cupboards. There was even a modern cookstove.

"Come I'll show you the office."

She followed him to a sizeable room with plenty of bookshelves, another fireplace and a big desk. Her eyes misted when she saw all the different fabric stacked on a shelf. On the next shelf there were every type of trimmings, lace, and ribbons of all colors. She couldn't help but touch the fabrics. "I've never seen the like."

"Let me show you the upstairs." Once again, She took her hand as he led her up the grand stairs. He showed her each room and they were all beautiful; light and airy except for MJ's he insisted his be navy blue. MJ jumped onto his bed and put his arm under his head, appearing very comfortable.

"Come this way." There was something soft and gentle about Murphy's voice.

He led them to a very spacious room with an enormous bed. The headboard was carved. She sat on the bed and traced her fingers over the words. *"I am my beloved's and my beloved is mine."*

"Oh my, this is absolutely beautiful!" She stood and kissed him.

"I have one more surprise." He grinned.

"More?"

Murphy took two rings out of his pocket. "I have mine and I bought you a new one." He took her hand and placed the ring on her finger. "Never have I known such love. All the time we missed distresses me but our love is stronger than ever."

Brooke took the other ring and put it on Murphy's finger. "I never thought to be loved the way you love me. We are so blessed; we have our hearts joined as one and we have an astonishing son. May we have a long time to make up for the lost years. And may God always walk with us."

ABOUT THE AUTHOR

Sexy Cowboys and the Women Who Love Them...
Finalist in the 2012 and 2015 RONE Awards.
Top Pick, Five Star Series from the Romance Review.
Kathleen Ball writes contemporary and historical western romance with great emotion and
memorable characters. Her books are award winners and have appeared on best sellers lists including: Amazon's Best Seller's List, All Romance Ebooks, Bookstrand, Desert Breeze Publishing and Secret Cravings Publishing Best Sellers list. She is the recipient of eight Editor's Choice Awards, and The Readers' Choice Award for Ryelee's Cowboy.
Winner of the Lear diamond award Best Historical Novel- Cinders' Bride
There's something about a cowboy

facebook.com/kathleenballwesternromance
twitter.com/kballauthor
instagram.com/author_kathleenball

OTHER BOOKS BY KATHLEEN

Lasso Spring Series
Callie's Heart
Lone Star Joy
Stetson's Storm

Dawson Ranch Series
Texas Haven
Ryelee's Cowboy

Cowboy Season Series
Summer's Desire
Autumn's Hope
Winter's Embrace
Spring's Delight

Mail Order Brides of Texas
Cinder's Bride
Keegan's Bride
Shane's Bride
Tramp's Bride
Poor Boy's Christmas

Oregon Trail Dreamin'
We've Only Just Begun
A Lifetime to Share
A Love Worth Searching For

So Many Roads to Choose

The Settlers
Greg

Juan

Scarlett

Mail Order Brides of Spring Water
Tattered Hearts

Shattered Trust

Glory's Groom

Battered Soul

Romance on the Oregon Trail
Cora's Courage

Luella's Longing

Dawn's Destiny

Terra's Trial

Candle Glow and Mistletoe

The Kabvanagh Brothers
Teagan: Cowboy Strong

Quinn: Cowboy Risk

Brogan: Cowboy Pride

Sullivan: Cowboy Protector

Donnell: Cowboy Scrutiny

Murphy: Cowboy Deceived

Fitzpatrick: Cowboy Reluctant

Angus: Cowboy Bewildered

The Greatest Gift

Love So Deep

Luke's Fate

Whispered Love

Love Before Midnight

I'm Forever Yours

Finn's Fortune

Glory's Groom

Made in the USA
Las Vegas, NV
21 October 2020